Main Street

Keeping Secrets

Also by Ann M. Martin

Belle Teal

A Corner of the Universe

A Dog's Life

Here Today

On Christmas Eve

P.S. Longer Letter Later
written with Paula Danziger

Snail Mail No More
written with Paula Danziger

Ten Kids, No Pets

The Baby-sitters Club series

Main Street #1: *Welcome to Camden Falls*

Main Street #2: *Needle and Thread*

Main Street #3: *'Tis the Season*

Main Street #4: *Best Friends*

Main Street #5: *The Secret Book Club*

Main Street #6: *September Surprises*

Main Street

Keeping Secrets

Ann M. Martin

SCHOLASTIC INC.

NEW YORK ◇ TORONTO ◇ LONDON ◇ AUCKLAND ◇ SYDNEY
MEXICO CITY ◇ NEW DELHI ◇ HONG KONG ◇ BUENOS AIRES

ISBN-13: 978-0-439-86885-3
ISBN-10: 0-439-86885-8

Illustrations by Dan Andreason

12 11 10 9 8 7 6 5 4 3 2 1   9 10 11 12 13 14/0

Printed in the U.S.A.

First printing, April 2009

Main Street

Keeping Secrets

Camden Falls

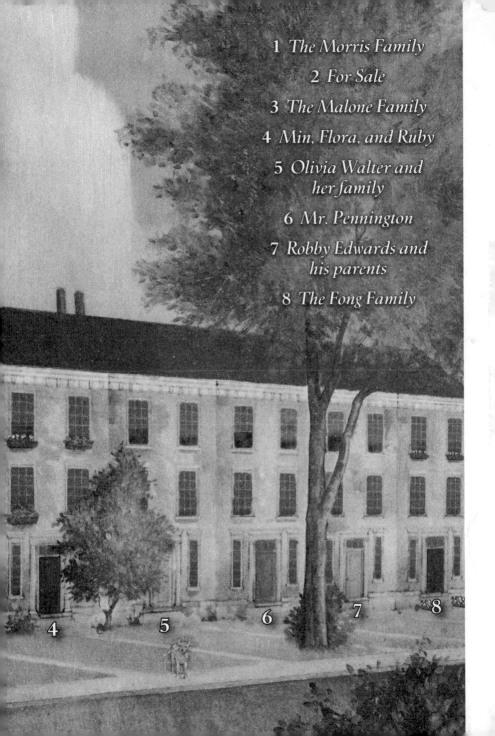

CHAPTER I

Changes

On an afternoon in early October, the sun shone down on Aiken Avenue in Camden Falls, Massachusetts. It shone on the Row Houses and their small tidy yards and on the children of the seven families who occupied the eight attached homes. The second house from the left, formerly the home of Bill and Mary Lou Willet, was currently without an owner. But it wouldn't be empty for long. The FOR SALE sign that had stood staunchly in the front yard for four weeks and three days (Flora had counted) was gone. Everyone wondered who would be moving in, and when. It had been a long time since there had been a new family in the Row Houses.

Flora Northrop, sitting on her front stoop, pushed Grace Fong's stroller lazily back and forth with her foot and considered changes. She had recently decided that life was a continuous series of changes, which was unfortunate, since she didn't like change. No, that wasn't true, Flora realized as she watched Grace gaze up and down the street with the wonder of a seven-month-old. Some changes were welcome and exciting. Grace's birth, for instance. A new baby at the Row Houses was a very welcome event. And Flora had been excited about leaving elementary school behind in the spring and entering seventh grade in the big central school in September. Two fine changes.

"Hey, guess what!" called Lacey Morris, galloping across the lawns to Flora and Grace.

"Just twenty-six days until Halloween!" announced Ruby, who was at Lacey's heels.

Lacey glared at Ruby. "*I* was going to tell her."

"Well," said Ruby, "the, um, important thing is that she knows."

"Huh," said Lacey.

Flora raised her eyebrows at her younger sister. "Ruby, remember what Min told you about hogging conversations."

"To do it?" said Ruby, and Lacey giggled.

"Anyway," said Flora. "Only twenty-six days? That's pretty exciting."

"I'm going to be a scarecrow," said Lacey.

"I'll be your crow," said Ruby.

"What are you going to be, Flora?" asked Lacey.

"I'm not sure —" Flora started to answer. She glanced up as the door to Olivia's house banged open, and Olivia and Nikki ran across the yard.

"Ooh," said Nikki, stopping to stroke Grace's fine hair, "she's so cute!"

Olivia stood back, hands on her hips, and glared at Flora. "Is this going to be a regular baby-sitting job?" she asked.

Flora shrugged. "I don't think so. Mrs. Fong just asked me to sit today."

"Why didn't she ask *me*?" said Olivia, frowning.

"Probably because you're too young," said Ruby, and Olivia made a face at her.

"Girls, girls," said Flora.

"So what about your Halloween costume?" Lacey asked again.

"Hey, maybe you guys could be farm animals," said Ruby. "Except one of you could be the farmer. Get it? A farmer, a scarecrow, a —"

"We get it," said Olivia.

"But," said Flora, "I'm not sure we're going to go trick-or-treating this year."

"*What?*" cried Ruby. "What do you mean? You *have* to go!"

Flora, Olivia, and Nikki exchanged glances.

"We're just not sure —" Flora began.

"We might be too old —" said Nikki.

"Just because you're in seventh grade . . ." Ruby muttered. She crossed her arms. "You'll change your minds," she said.

As Flora watched Lacey drift back to her house, she

recalled the previous Halloween. She and Ruby had been living in Camden Falls for just four months. She had been a whole year younger, but sometimes she had felt like the oldest person in the world, older even than Min, her grandmother. That Halloween had been one of the first holidays she and Ruby had spent without their parents. Maybe, Flora thought now, it was a good thing Halloween in Camden Falls was celebrated so differently from Halloween in the town in which she and Ruby had grown up. There, kids just went trick-or-treating up and down the streets in their neighborhoods. Here, some kids did that, but most wound up on Main Street, trick-or-treating at the stores.

Changes, Flora thought again. She lifted Grace out of her stroller and sat her in her lap. The very biggest change in Flora's life — Flora knew with absolute certainty that no matter how long she lived, she would experience no bigger change — had occurred on a snowy night in January almost two years earlier. That was when the car in which she and Ruby had been riding with their parents had collided with a truck, and the lives of Mr. and Mrs. Northrop had been taken immediately. Min, their busy grandmother (Min was short both for Mindy and for "in a minute"), had arrived that very night and had taken care of Flora and Ruby until the end of the school year. But as soon as school was over, she had packed up their things and moved them to Camden Falls to live in the house in which their mother and Min herself had grown up.

This change, Flora knew, was certainly not all bad. Of course, if she could somehow have her parents and her old life back, if she could reverse time and stay home on that stormy night, she would do it. No question. But all things considered, her new life in Camden Falls was more than satisfactory. She and Ruby lived next door to Olivia in the Row Houses, and Olivia Walter was one of her best friends. Nikki Sherman was her other best friend. Flora was grateful to have made good friends so quickly. Furthermore, Olivia's grandmother and Min owned Needle and Thread, a sewing store on Main Street. How many girls who loved to sew, as Flora did, had a grandmother with a sewing store? Flora knew she should count her lucky stars.

"Hey, where's Robby?" Ruby asked suddenly, the subject of Halloween costumes apparently forgotten.

"Mom and Dad gave him more hours at the store," Olivia told her.

"Really? That's great," said Nikki.

Olivia's parents had recently opened a store, Sincerely Yours, on Main Street, not far from Needle and Thread. One of the first people they had hired to work in the store was Robby Edwards, who lived in the second to the last Row House on the right. Robby, who was eighteen and had Down syndrome, had graduated from high school in June and then proudly started his new job.

"He must be really happy," said Flora.

"*You* don't sound happy," said Ruby. "What's the matter?"

Flora shrugged. "I was thinking about changes," she said. She shifted Grace in her lap.

Olivia and Nikki plopped down on the stoop on either side of Flora, but Ruby cocked her head and frowned. "Again? We've already had this discussion."

"You could be a little more supportive," Nikki said, and put her arm around her friend.

"Well, Ruby's right, actually," said Flora.

"Thank you," said Ruby contritely.

"Remember when *I* was the one who didn't want things to change?" said Olivia.

"Change is hard for lots of people," Nikki pointed out. "But think of all the good changes."

"That's what I've been saying!" said Ruby.

Olivia replaced one of the barrettes in her wild hair. "Actually, I still wish certain things could stay the same forever. I wish Mr. and Mrs. Willet hadn't moved away."

"Me, too," said Flora.

"But aren't you excited about getting new neighbors?" asked Ruby. "Maybe it will be a family with ten kids! The youngest one could be Grace's age, so she wouldn't be the only baby in the Row Houses. Then there could be, like, a five-year-old for Alyssa Morris, a few boys for all the brothers around here, a girl for Lacey and me, some teenagers for Robby and for Lydia and Margaret Malone, and a cute boy for you guys to drool over."

"We do not drool!" exclaimed Nikki.

"Well, anyway, Olivia already has a boyfriend," Ruby said smugly. "Olivia and Jacob, sitting in a tree, K-I-S-S —"

"Jacob is not my boyfriend!" cried Olivia.

"Or maybe," continued Ruby, as if she hadn't heard either Olivia or Nikki, "it will be a young couple and the woman is pregnant and she gives birth to six-tuplets, or whatever you call six babies, and a TV station wants to do a show about them, and we all get to be in it. Just think — week after week of TV cameras everywhere. I would make sure to practice my tap routines on the sidewalk so I could get discovered."

Flora shook her head. Some things about Ruby would *never* change. Ruby saw her sister's expression and turned on her. "It could happen —" she started to say.

But she was interrupted by Lacey's brothers, Travis and Mathias, and Olivia's brothers, Jack and Henry, running across the yards toward them, Alyssa trailing behind.

"Nikki!" called Henry Walter. "We're glad you're here. We have a question. Can we be in the dog parade if we don't have a dog?"

Over the summer, Nikki had come up with the idea of holding a dog costume parade on Main Street as a way to raise money for Camden Falls's animal shelter. The people who ran Sheltering Arms had taken over the project (to Nikki's relief, since it was a very big project), but everyone knew that Nikki was the one who had thought it up. And everyone wanted to be in it. Flora and Ruby were going to enter Daisy Dear, their golden retriever.

Nikki frowned. "How could you be in a dog parade without a dog?" she asked.

"Well, what if one of us dressed up *as* a dog?" suggested Mathias.

"Or as a dog in a costume?" said Jack. "Henry could put on a dog costume, and we could put a clown costume or something over *that*, and then I could put him on a leash and walk him in the parade."

"You mean Henry would crawl on his hands and knees all the way down Main Street?" said Olivia.

"Oh," said Jack and Henry.

"We didn't think of that," added Travis.

"We should probably stick to actual dogs in the parade. Besides," said Nikki, "we also need people to *watch* the parade. Don't you guys want to see all the dogs in funny costumes?"

"Hey," said Mathias. "There's Mr. Pennington and Jacques. I'll bet Mr. Pennington is going to walk Jacques in the parade."

"I could help him with the costume!" said Flora, brightening.

"Hi, Mr. Pennington!" called Ruby.

Old Mr. Pennington locked his front door (he lived next to Olivia and her brothers) and waved to the kids. "I'm off to Needle and Thread," he called as he stumped down the walk with his cane in one hand and Jacques's leash in the other.

"To visit Min?" said Ruby with a grin.

"Of course."

Flora felt something in her stomach tighten just the teensiest bit. She loved Mr. Pennington. He had been a good friend to her and Ruby and Min. But his longtime friendship with Min was becoming . . . Flora wasn't certain how to describe it. She found that she was rather clueless in matters of the heart. And her feelings were jumbled. What, exactly, did that tightening in her stomach mean? Was it jealousy? If it was, who was she jealous of? Min for having a boyfriend, or Mr. Pennington for having Min's attention? Both possibilities seemed at once silly and monumental.

Mr. Pennington and Jacques made their way slowly along Aiken Avenue, the younger children walking beside him, presumably questioning him about Jacques's participation in the parade.

Ruby flopped onto the stoop next to Flora. "Move over," she said.

Flora, Nikki, and Olivia squeezed together, and Flora returned Grace to her stroller.

"Hey!" Olivia held up one hand. "Is that our phone? I think our phone is ringing." She jumped to her feet and made a dash for her front door.

"Ha! It's probably Jacob," proclaimed Ruby.

Flora stared sullenly at nothing and said not a word when Olivia, smiling, returned to the stoop and exclaimed, "That was Jacob! We're going to do our homework together over the phone tonight."

Flora remembered the times *she* and Olivia had done their homework over the phone. She remembered when Mr. Pennington was just Min's dear friend, and when she didn't have to think about whether to go trick-or-treating. She let her thoughts meander through her head, and when they settled on sewing, Flora found her mood improving. Making dog costumes would be fun. What could she make for Jacques? What could she and Ruby make for Daisy? Maybe they could dress her as a daisy. That seemed appropriate. Flora considered daisy petals and leaves. She began a shopping list in her head. Yellow felt, green felt, elastic, probably some Velcro . . .

CHAPTER 2

Dogs

From a distance, and in the fading light of an autumn afternoon, Nikki Sherman thought her house looked rather nice. It sat alone in the countryside, a small island in a sea of earth and grass. It was only as a person drew closer that he might see the dilapidated sheds in the yard and notice that the yard itself, unlike the ones in town, consisted mostly of hard-packed dry earth, and that around the perimeter of the yard, wild stalky grasses stretched away in all directions.

Nikki hurried along her lane as the school bus wheezed back in the direction of Camden Falls. The nearer she got to her house, the more clearly she could see all the disappointing, run-down details: the sagging steps of the front stoop, the peeling paint, the mark by the side window where her father had once thrown a board at her brother. (He had missed, luckily.) But Nikki loved her house anyway. She and Tobias and Mae had grown up in it. They knew no other home.

And with her father away (permanently, Nikki hoped), her home was even more pleasing.

Still, it would be nice to come home to people at the end of a school day, and that didn't happen anymore. Nikki's mother had finally landed a big job, the kind her husband had told her she'd never qualify for, but it came with long hours. And because Mrs. Sherman didn't want Nikki to feel responsible for her little sister, she had kept Mae in after-school day care. So no more Dad, Mom at work, Mae in day care — and Tobias off at college, which was something no one had expected, least of all Tobias. He was the first Sherman to go to college, and the day he graduated and held that diploma in his hand would be a proud day indeed, a day to go down in Sherman family history.

Nikki herself would go to college one day. She knew that with certainty, in the same way she knew her name. She had dreamed of college for as long as she could remember, and now that Tobias was a college student, her dream seemed nearer than ever.

"Six years," she said to herself. "In six years, I'll be in college."

Nikki climbed the porch steps, set her books at her feet, and pulled her house key from her pocket. From the other side of the door she heard snuffling and a quiet whine.

Nikki grinned. "Hi, Paw-Paw!" she cried.

The whine turned to a plaintive *woof*, and then another.

"I'm coming," Nikki said, working the lock as fast as she could.

She pushed the door open, and Paw-Paw jumped up, resting his feet on Nikki's belly, trembling with excitement.

"Hello, boy," Nikki said softly. She gave him a great hug. "I'm hungry. And I'll bet you need to go outside."

Paw-Paw bolted through the door. Nikki had gotten no further than opening the refrigerator when she heard the sound of tires on gravel. She peered through the front window. A white van was easing up the driveway, and Nikki could read the words on its side: SHELTERING ARMS.

She breathed a sigh of relief. She hadn't known someone from Sheltering Arms would be coming this afternoon, but it was fine with her. She abandoned the idea of a snack and went outside.

A woman was climbing out of the van, and she waved to Nikki. "Hello!"

"Hi, Harriet!" Nikki called.

Paw-Paw ran to Harriet and gave her the same enthusiastic greeting he had just given Nikki.

"So, how are things?" asked Harriet, disengaging herself from Paw-Paw.

"Good," replied Nikki. "Really good. I like school. We get a lot of homework, though."

"And the dogs?"

Nikki knew that Harriet meant the stray dogs that hung around the Shermans' yard. They came nearly every day, usually early in the morning and again in the evening, just as darkness was falling. Nikki fed them but couldn't afford to do much more for them. The previous fall, when so many dogs had been coming by (Paw-Paw was one of them) that Nikki couldn't keep up with them, she had finally asked the people at Sheltering Arms for help, and since then, they had come by regularly. Often they brought a supply of food for the dogs. And sometimes they set up humane traps for them, brought them back to the shelter, spayed or neutered them, gave them medical attention, and kept the ones they felt were adoptable. The feral ones were returned to continue living on their own. Nikki was grateful, and she very much liked everyone she had met at the shelter.

"There aren't very many of them," she told Harriet now. "Lately, I've only seen four dogs."

"Excellent," said Harriet. "Spaying and neutering is the key. Do you need anything?"

"More dry food, if you have it," said Nikki uncomfortably. She had felt like a charity case many times in her life, and accepting donations didn't come easily.

Harriet laughed. "*If* we have it!" she said. "Nikki, come take a look in the van."

Nikki peered through the back doors. She counted eleven enormous bags of chow.

"You're my sixth stop today, and I have two more to go. Believe me, we're grateful to people like you who help strays."

Nikki smiled.

Harriet heaved a bag of food out of the van. *"Oof."* She straightened up. "So, is Paw-Paw going to walk in the dog parade?"

"Definitely. I promised Mae we'd make his costume soon."

"The newspaper ad is going to run at the end of the week," said Harriet. "Five dollars to enter the parade, and everyone who comes to watch will be encouraged to contribute. We'll have volunteers up and down Main Street with canisters for donations. Did you see the posters? We put them up on October first. Nikki, you had a wonderful idea."

"Thank you," said Nikki, patting Paw-Paw and looking at the ground.

Harriet gazed across the Shermans' yard. "Are you concerned about any of the dogs that are coming by?" she asked.

"Well," said Nikki thoughtfully, "three of them look okay. You know, scruffy and they probably have some fleas, but basically okay. The fourth one is limping, though. And I think she has a tick on her neck."

"Will she let you get close to her?"

Nikki shook her head. "Nope. And I've tried lots of times."

"Do you think she's feral?"

"I don't know. Maybe not exactly feral. She doesn't run away from me. I think she might just be hand shy."

Harriet paused. Then she said, "I guess I should try to trap her."

"Okay." Nikki and Harriet both knew what that meant. Trapping a specific dog, even with a humane trap, wasn't as straightforward as it sounded. Any kind of animal could wind up in the trap, including one of the other dogs. Once, Harriet had set a trap, and later that day Nikki found Paw-Paw sitting grouchily in it.

"Will you be able to check the trap tonight and again tomorrow before you leave for school?" asked Harriet. "I'll want to come pick up the dog as soon as possible."

"I'll make time," said Nikki.

Harriet grinned. "I can't ask for more."

Nikki and Harriet set the trap, placing a dog biscuit at the back and carefully setting the door so that it would shut — and lock — behind the dog when she nosed inside for the treat. Then Nikki called good-bye to Harriet, returned to the house, and sat down at the kitchen table, her schoolbooks stacked beside her, Paw-Paw dozing at her feet. She was reading an amazingly dull paragraph about the French Revolution for what she estimated was the seventh time when the phone rang, startling her and causing Paw-Paw to leap to his feet, barking mightily.

"Thank you for protecting me from the telephone," Nikki said to him as she pressed the TALK button. "Hello?"

"Hello; little sis."

"Tobias!"

"How's everything?"

"Great. But I miss you."

"I miss you, too. Is Mom there?"

"Nope. No one else is home yet."

"Oh." Tobias sounded disappointed. "I didn't look at the time before I called."

"Is something going on?"

"Something good."

"What? What?"

"What are you guys doing the first weekend in November?"

"I don't know. Why?"

"I just found out that the first Saturday in November is family visiting day at Leavitt. I was hoping you and Mom and Mae could come."

Nikki let out a small shriek. "Yes! Yes, oh, yes, oh, yes! Come visit you at college? I've been waiting for this! I want to see everything! I want to see your dorm and the science center — didn't you say there's a greenhouse? — and the library and the theatre —" Nikki could hear Tobias laughing. "I want to see everything!" she exclaimed again.

"Do you think Mom has to work that day?"

"I don't know, but it's a month away. I'm sure she can figure something out. Then it'll just be . . ." Nikki's voice trailed off.

"I know," said Tobias.

Nikki sighed. "For starters, she'll have to drive to a strange place."

"I'll give you directions."

"And I'll get maps," said Nikki. "But also . . . Mom will feel out of place at Leavitt." Nikki thought of her mother, whose parents had barely allowed her to graduate from high school. For her, college had been out of the question, not even a consideration. Nikki knew Mrs. Sherman was proud of Tobias. She also knew her mother felt he had entered a world that was as foreign to her as Greece (a country Nikki hoped to visit one day). "She'll be afraid she won't fit in with the other college parents."

"I know. I mean, I know that's how she'll feel. We'll have to handle this very delicately."

"With finesse," said Nikki.

"With tact," said Tobias.

"Maybe I could bribe her," said Nikki, and Tobias laughed again.

"I'll call back tonight and talk to her," said Tobias. "I want to show you all around the campus, and we could have lunch in the student center."

Nikki closed her eyes and imagined visiting a college town and touring an actual college campus. She imagined meeting Tobias's roommates and walking under a wrought iron archway that read LEAVITT COLLEGE. She didn't know how she and Tobias were going to convince their mother to make the trip, but she knew they had to make it happen somehow.

CHAPTER 3

A Peek in the Windows

Camden Falls, Massachusetts, puts on appropriate finery for every season of the year. In winter, icicles glisten from under the eaves and green wreaths appear on red doors. In spring, the trees are tinged with a breathtaking pale green, the exact shade as young grasshoppers. In summer, hydrangeas puff out, fat as cotton candy, lavender and blue and white. And in autumn, Main Street is lined with grinning orange jack-o'-lanterns, and Mr. Freedly comes by to fasten sheaves of bristling cornstalks to the lampposts.

If you were to walk down Main Street on an afternoon in early October, you would see signs of autumn and Halloween and Thanksgiving on the sidewalks and in the stores and even on some of the people who pass by. There's Alyssa Morris, a proud kindergartner, walking hand in hand with her mother. On her head, Alyssa wears a paper crown decorated with ghosts and black cats that she made with her beloved art teacher at Camden Falls Elementary earlier today.

Peek in the shop windows and you'll see candy corn and strings of pumpkin lights and mechanical monsters (one of which terrified Alyssa last autumn, but she won't fall for that now). In the window of Sincerely Yours, the shop owned by Olivia's family, is a tray of candy apple witches. In the window of Needle and Thread is an array of Halloween costumes (some for dogs), the supplies for which can be purchased inside. The windows of Frank's Beans, the coffee shop, are draped with orange and brown crepe paper, and in each corner sits a cardboard turkey.

This is Main Street in Camden Falls at the start of another October. The days are noticeably shorter now, and as Alyssa and her mother pass College Pizza, Mrs. Morris says, "Goodness, it's starting to get dark. Time to go home."

If you were to walk with the Morrises now, you would find that their home is just a few minutes away. At the end of the block, turn left on Dodds Lane, then turn right on Aiken Avenue, and ahead on your left you'll see the Row Houses. Alyssa has lived in the Row Houses for her entire life, but she's just five and the Row Houses were built more than one hundred and twenty years before she was born. The huge granite structure is unlike anything else in Camden Falls. The eight three-story homes were once owned by wealthy families with maids and chauffeurs, and are now owned by a variety of families, some with children, some with pets, some with children and pets, but absolutely no one with a maid or a chauffeur.

Darkness is falling fast now, and Alyssa and her mother hurry into their house. Lights are blinking on in the Row Houses and in windows up and down Aiken Avenue and beyond. Behind the windows, in rooms of all sizes and colors and shapes, the people of Camden Falls are living their lives. When the Morrises enter their home, Mrs. Morris turns on the lights in the living room and then the ones in the kitchen. The three older Morris children are at after-school activities and Mr. Morris is still at work. "Come help me fix dinner," Mrs. Morris says to Alyssa, and Alyssa carefully removes her crown. She wants it to stay fresh and clean, since she plans to keep it her entire life.

Next door to the Morrises, the Willets' old house sits in darkness, awaiting its new owners. In the house next to that, the Malones', one window on the second floor glows softly. Behind this window sits Margaret Malone, busily working away at her college applications and wondering where her younger sister is. Lydia has been grounded by Dr. Malone and was supposed to come home directly after school.

On the other side of the Malones' house is the one belonging to Min, Flora, and Ruby. In this house, lights are on everywhere. Min is still working at Needle and Thread, but Ruby and Flora are at home, and Ruby turned on the light in the kitchen when she got a snack, and then the light in the living room when she was looking for her socks, and then the light in the dining room when she stooped to pat her cat, King Comma (who was napping under the table), and then the light in the bathroom, which she forgot to turn off on her way out, and finally the light in her bedroom, where she is now practicing for tomorrow's rehearsal of the Camden Falls Children's Chorus. *"Every honeybee . . . fills with jealousy!"* sings Ruby. She's very excited about the next performance by the chorus, which will be a revue of songs by Fats Waller.

Across the hall from Ruby, Flora is sitting on her floor. Her schoolbooks are stacked on her desk and she supposes she should be doing her homework, but her mind is on a few other things. Spread around her on the floor are several pieces of fabric recently purchased at Needle and Thread (Min gives Flora a discount on N & T merchandise but will not allow her to bring things home for free) — three patterns, all for vests; several cards of buttons; and two patterns for making costumes for medium-size dogs. Flora is trying to concentrate, both on the vests and on Daisy's daisy costume, but her thoughts keep wandering, mostly to Min and Mr. Pennington. What would you call them? Girlfriend and boyfriend? Speaking of which, is Jacob really Olivia's boyfriend now? Are Min and Mr. Pennington young enough to be considered girlfriend and boyfriend? Are Olivia and Jacob old enough to be considered girlfriend and boyfriend? Why doesn't Flora have a boyfriend yet? Does she want one?

Flora makes a face. She reaches for the vest patterns and places them in a row in front of her. Then she holds one above a length of plaid fabric. Usually, this is Flora's favorite part of any project — the planning stage. But right now she just can't concentrate.

"Ruby?" Flora calls.

"Two sleepy people by dawn's early light!" sings Ruby.

Flora tries to focus on the vests.

Next door to Flora, Olivia's house is busy. Her mother has just returned from Sincerely Yours, and Olivia and her brothers are beginning their homework. Olivia is patiently working through a math problem when she hears the phone ring. Seconds later, Jack calls, "Olivia, it's your boyfriend!"

Leave the Row Houses now and walk through Camden Falls to the house purchased earlier this year by Flora and Ruby's aunt Allie, a writer. Allie is something of a mystery to Flora and Ruby. She's a bit hard to get to know (although she tries hard where her nieces are concerned), and just a few weeks earlier Flora and Ruby came across a closet full of brand-new baby clothes in her house. They found that particularly interesting since Allie is single. Here she is now, sitting in her study in front of her computer. She saves the changes she made to her new novel and turns to her e-mail. Her eyes widen when she sees the screen address pmaulden. Paul. She hasn't heard from Paul since she left New York City to return to Camden Falls. She can actually feel her chest tighten as she clicks on his name.

If you were to leave town now and travel several miles out on the county road, you'd come to the home of Nikki Sherman. She and her mother and Mae are sitting together on the couch, unwinding in front of the television for a few minutes before it's time for supper and homework and baths and stories. "Mom?" says Nikki tentatively. "Did you have a chance to think about the trip to Leavitt yet?"

Several miles from Camden Falls in a different direction lies Three Oaks, the retirement community where Mr. and Mrs. Willet now live. They live separately, since Mrs. Willet resides in the wing for people with Alzheimer's, and Mr. Willet has his own apartment. But Mr. Willet is relieved and happy to be just minutes from his wife instead of miles. It's almost dinnertime now, and Mr. Willet is getting ready to go downstairs to the dining room. He likes the dining room, but he can't help thinking longingly of his old house on Aiken Avenue.

Sixty-four miles from Camden Falls, in another small town, this one in New Hampshire, Willow Hamilton, who recently turned twelve, looks around her bedroom. For two days she has been methodically packing up the things in her room. She has insisted on doing this by herself. She doesn't want help, particularly not her mother's. It's bad enough that downstairs in the kitchen her mother has insisted on washing absolutely every item before she places it in a packing carton. She will, Willow knows, wash each item again before it can be put away in the new house. There's a hollow feeling in Willow's stomach, as if something bad is on the horizon. She closes her eyes and tries to picture her new home on Aiken Avenue.

CHAPTER 4

Melody

A
Halloween
Dance

Olivia Walter rolled out of bed, crossed her room, and looked at the calendar over her desk. Olivia was able to go from sound asleep to wide-awake in a matter of seconds — when she felt like it. Sometimes, especially on a weekend morning, Olivia would wake briefly, then curl into a ball and slip farther down toward the end of her bed, her entire body under the covers. But often, Olivia heard her alarm go off, and — *bing!* — she was awake. That had happened on this October morning, and the moment her eyes were open, she thought about her birthday and the fact that in a little under a month she would finally turn eleven. True, some of her classmates had already turned thirteen, but at least Olivia (who had skipped second grade) would be able to stop saying she was ten.

Olivia released a massive sigh as she remembered the year before, when she couldn't wait to turn ten — to have two numbers in her age and to celebrate her big one-oh. Now all she wanted was to be another year older.

Olivia was moving so fast that by the time she finished letting out her sigh she was already standing in front of her desk, looking at the November page on her wall calendar. She counted the days until her eleventh birthday. Just under thirty. Not bad. She decided she didn't even care about a party this year. Simply turning eleven would be exciting enough.

If she could have a birthday wish, just a single little wish — one that was guaranteed to come true, of course — she knew what it would be. She would wish that Melody Becker and Tanya Rhodes had never been born. Wait a minute. *That* sounded a bit harsh. Maybe she should rephrase her wish. She considered this as she opened her wardrobe and scanned her sweaters. Perhaps what she meant was that she would wish Melody and Tanya weren't mean to her. That sounded better, although a bit flimsy. Didn't she really wish that they were, in fact, nice to her? No, not necessarily. Well, maybe.

What she wished for was no trouble at school.

Olivia selected a sweater, a shirt, and a pair of jeans. Her thoughts were a jumble. In the same moment that she was thinking about a world in which Melody and Tanya were nice to her, she was also wondering if they would see her outfit today and make fun of it. It wouldn't be the first time. Didn't they understand how difficult it was to find sophisticated-looking clothes when she was forced to shop in the children's department? (Not only was Olivia still ten, she was small for her age.)

"A pox on Melody and Tanya," said Olivia aloud. "Especially on Melody."

Melody was Olivia's nemesis, a word she had discovered recently in a mystery story.

"A pox!" said Olivia more loudly.

"Olivia?" called her mother from the hallway. "Everything all right in there?"

"Yes," answered Olivia, and she could feel herself blushing.

She saw her sneakers by the bed, jammed them onto her feet, and headed for the bathroom, grateful that Melody and Tanya could be balanced — outweighed, actually — by all the good things in her life, especially Nikki, Flora, and Ruby, her true friends.

The year before, back when Olivia still went to Camden Falls Elementary, she and Flora and Ruby had walked to school together every day and waited outside to meet Nikki's bus. This year, Olivia, Flora, and Ruby could walk together only one block, to the point at which Aiken Avenue intersected with Dodds Lane. There, Ruby turned right, heading for the elementary school, usually side by side with Lacey Morris, while Olivia and Flora turned left to continue their walk to the central school on the other side of town, where once again they would meet Nikki's bus.

"There she is," said Flora that morning, as a line of students, some of them looking very sleepy, was disgorged from a Camden Falls Central School District bus.

"Hi!" Nikki called as she ran to her friends. "Guess what."

"What?" said Olivia. "Something good?"

"Yup. My mom said we can visit Tobias next month."

"Really? That's great!" said Flora.

"I know." Nikki grinned. "She's nervous about it, but she's going to do it. And I'll get to see a real college."

The girls joined the students streaming through the front entrance of their school. Olivia never ceased to be impressed by some of the oldest students, the ones in eleventh and twelfth grades. Would she ever — *ever* — be as tall or as, well, *shapely* as they were? She glanced down at her perfectly flat chest and stick-straight body. It didn't seem likely.

"Hey!" said Flora. "Look at that."

Olivia and Nikki turned in the direction in which Flora was pointing, and along one wall of the main hallway saw an enormous hand-lettered sign announcing . . .

"A Halloween dance," said Nikki.

"For seventh- and eighth-graders," said Flora.

"Our first school dance," said Olivia. "Actually, our first dance ever. Mine, anyway."

"Mine, too," said Nikki and Flora.

Olivia now read the entire sign. "'Camden Falls Central High School presents the annual Halloween dance for seventh- and eighth-graders. Halloween night. Six to nine o'clock. Food! Music! Fun! No costume necessary.'"

The girls looked at one another.

"Our first dance ever," Olivia said again.

"Should we go?" asked Nikki.

"We don't need costumes," said Flora. "I don't know whether that's good or bad. What should we wear instead?"

"Yeah. I wonder if people get dressed up," said Nikki.

"In evening gowns," said Olivia, and the others laughed.

"Gosh," said Flora. "Dancing with boys. I'm not sure I want to dance with boys."

"Sometimes girls all dance together in a group," said Nikki. "I've seen that on television. Boy, it's a good thing my father isn't around anymore. He'd never let me go to a dance."

"Your mother will let you go, though, won't she?" Olivia asked anxiously.

"Definitely. I think she'll be excited about it."

"How dressed up *do* we get?" Olivia wondered aloud, and it was while she was waiting for an answer that she became aware of voices behind her.

"Should we get out our ball gowns?" someone said.

"Right after we make sure our pumpkin coach is available," someone else replied.

The first voice became high and adopted an unconvincing British accent. "Oh, Maximilian, how *chah*-ming of you to invite me.... What? A rose corsage? ... Oh, no, darling, that isn't necessary."

Olivia closed her eyes. The voices, derisive and sarcastic, belonged to Melody Becker and Tanya Rhodes. She didn't need to turn around to know that. She could even tell that Melody was the first speaker and Tanya the second. Tanya was rude and thoughtless, but Melody — Melody was out-and-out mean. Almost as soon as school had gotten under way in September, Melody had tried to take advantage of Olivia by enlisting her to help with her homework (okay, to do it for her). Olivia, at first pleased to have been befriended by someone as popular and sophisticated as Melody, soon realized she was being taken advantage of. And she'd worked hard to outwit her. ("What did Melody expect?" Ruby had said later. "She was using you because you're smart and she needed your brainpower. Didn't it occur to her that you would use that brainpower to get back at her?")

Olivia opened her eyes and glanced first at Nikki, then at Flora. She was about to say that maybe she was hallucinating — she was hearing the voices of stupid people in her head — when behind her Melody whispered loudly, "She has nothing to worry about. No one will want to dance with a nine-year-old."

Olivia whirled around. "I am *not* nine —"

"Hey, you guys!" a cheerful voice called. "What's going on?"

Nikki poked Olivia and whispered, "Jacob's here."

"Hi, Olivia." Jacob smiled at her. "Hi, Flora. Hi, Nikki." He glanced at Tanya and Melody and said nothing. His eyes landed on Olivia again, and then he noticed the poster. "Cool! A dance!" He touched Olivia's arm. "I have to go. See you later." He strode down the hall.

Olivia looked after him. By the time he turned a corner, Tanya and Melody had disappeared.

"They slunk away like cats," announced Nikki with satisfaction. She paused. "Although I probably shouldn't say that. It's mean to cats."

Olivia laughed.

"*He* seemed pretty interested in the dance," said Flora.

"Melody seemed pretty interested in him," remarked Nikki.

"Yes. Unfortunately, he can't stand her. Poor, poor Melody," said Flora. "Well, that's what she gets for being a, um, a . . ."

"A toad?" suggested Nikki.

"A worm?" suggested Olivia.

"Although, again, we don't want to be mean to toads or worms," said Nikki.

Much later, near the end of the day, Olivia and Nikki made a quick stop at Olivia's locker between classes.

"What's that?" asked Nikki, and she pointed to a slip of white paper sticking out of the door.

"Oh, no. Not again," said Olivia with a moan. She plucked the paper from the crack and held it between her thumb and forefinger as if she had just pulled it from a garbage can. "I'm going to throw it away without reading it. Melody's probably watching from somewhere. Won't she be surprised if I don't even look at it?"

"What if it's from Jacob?" asked Nikki.

"It isn't. Jacob always writes my name in fancy script. He'd never leave a plain old note like this." Olivia crumpled the paper, unread. "There," she said.

"What's the matter?" asked Nikki. "I know something's still bothering you."

"Well . . . she found my new locker!" exclaimed Olivia. "I thought I was safe from her."

"All she had to do was follow you. It wouldn't be hard to find anybody's locker."

"That's true." Olivia thought uncomfortably of her old locker, the one that had been broken and didn't actually lock. Melody had begun stealing Olivia's homework (always perfectly executed) out of the locker, copying it over, and handing it in as her own — until Olivia had caught on and outsmarted her.

"Anyway," said Nikki, "Melody can't get into *this* locker. That's the important thing. So you're still safe."

"True," replied Olivia. She smiled at Nikki, then tossed the crumpled note in a trash can. "Can't get me!" she exclaimed.

CHAPTER 5

Lions and Witches, Bears and Kittens

Lacey Morris's house was a mirror image of Ruby's. The same but backward, thought Ruby. This meant that although Lacey, like Ruby, occupied the room on the second floor opposite the top of the staircase, it was in fact on the other side of the house, and because the Morrises lived in one of the coveted end-of-the-row houses, Lacey had a corner bedroom featuring not only a window facing the front yard but one facing south as well. It was a bright, airy room, and Ruby was slightly jealous of it — a fact she did her best to hide.

"You know," said Ruby one afternoon as she and Hilary Nelson and Lacey sat in Lacey's sun-filled room, "we should really make a decision about our Halloween costumes right now and get started on them."

"Especially since we might need help with them," said Lacey.

"Yeah. We should give Min and Flora and your parents plenty of advance warning. Your parents, too, Hilary."

"Don't we want to make the costumes ourselves?" asked Hilary. She had moved to Camden Falls over the summer. This would be her first Halloween in her new town.

"People around here make costumes that are pretty, um — what's the word?" said Ruby.

"Fancy?" suggested Lacey.

"No . . ."

"Elaborate?" suggested Hilary.

"That's it. Elaborate," said Ruby. "Just wait until you go trick-or-treating on Main Street with us. Then you'll see. Even the people who run the stores get dressed up."

"What — you mean your *grandmother* gets dressed up?" asked Hilary incredulously.

"Yes. Hey, you have to tell your parents about this, Hilary," said Lacey with sudden urgency. "They'll have to decorate the diner. And —"

"Oh, no!" exclaimed Hilary. "I know what you're going to say. My mom and dad will have to get dressed up! Yipes."

The Nelsons — Mr. and Mrs. Nelson, Hilary (who was ten like Ruby), and Hilary's younger brother, Spencer — had moved to Camden Falls at the beginning of the summer. Hilary's parents had decided to leave Boston in order to raise their children in the quiet of a small town. They had sold their home and bought a small building on Main Street, one in which they planned both to live and to run a diner. They had been busily renovating the building, creating the Marquis Diner on the ground floor and converting the second story into their living quarters, when a middle-of-the-night fire damaged the building and nearly sent the Nelsons back to Boston. But the people of Camden Falls, inspired by an idea of Ruby's, had held Nelson Day, a fund-raiser that had made enough money to get Hilary's family back on their feet. Now the diner was open again, and practically everyone in Camden Falls knew the Nelsons. But the Nelsons were still learning about their new town.

"Won't your parents *want* to get dressed up?" Ruby asked Hilary.

"They're not very, um, dressy-up people. They're kind of shy." Hilary let her gaze travel out Lacey's front window, through which she could see the back of her apartment on Main Street and even make out her own bedroom window. "What does your grandmother wear on Halloween?" she asked, turning to Ruby.

"Every year she dresses as the Wicked Witch of the West from *The Wizard of Oz*. And Gigi dresses as Glinda, the Good Witch." (Gigi was Olivia's grandmother.) "Their costumes are really great."

"Hey, this year Olivia's parents will have to get dressed up, too," said Lacey. "This will be the first Halloween since Sincerely Yours opened."

"Well, anyway, let's think about our own costumes," said Ruby again. "So. What could we be?"

"I always wanted to be a Tibetan spaniel," said Hilary.

"A . . . what?" said Ruby and Lacey.

"It's a dog."

"Oh. I kind of want to be a clock," said Lacey. "A grandfather clock."

"Interesting," replied Ruby. "I was thinking about being an enormous pair of glasses, but that would be hard because the glasses would probably have to stand on end and they wouldn't look as good that way."

The girls sat in silence for a few moments.

"It might be more fun if we went as three things that go together," said Lacey. "You know, like the Three Bears."

"Or the Three Kings. The ones from Orient Are," said Ruby.

"Oh! Oh! How about the Lion, the Witch, and the Wardrobe?" suggested Hilary.

Ruby narrowed her eyes. "Which one of us would have to be the Wardrobe?"

"Well . . . not me, since it was my idea. I want to be the Witch."

"I call the Lion!" cried Ruby, jumping to her feet.

"Hey, who said we even decided on the Lion, the Witch, and the Wardrobe?" exclaimed Lacey. "What about the Three Bears?"

"Too babyish," said Ruby, and Lacey glared at her.

"Well, now, wait a minute," said Hilary. "There are plenty of things that go together. We just need to think."

"We could be three of a kind, from a deck of cards," said Ruby.

"Boring," said Lacey.

"How about the Three Little Pigs?" said Hilary.

"The Three Little Kittens, the ones that lost their mittens," said Ruby.

"Talk about babyish," remarked Lacey.

"Anyway, let's try to be more original," said Hilary. "Use our imaginations. We could be three any-things — three different kinds of candy bars."

"That could be fun," said Lacey.

"Three different kinds of flowers. A bouquet of flowers!"

"Ooh, I like that," said Lacey.

Ruby looked thoughtful. "I have an idea. What if we were three magic witches? Then we could have really fun costumes. We could be witches but with just a touch of magic." Ruby envisioned costumes calling for much sparkle and glitter, as well as magic wands and crowns in addition to normal witch attire.

"What are magic witches?" asked Hilary.

"Does it matter?"

"It might," said Lacey, frowning. "How will people know what we are?"

"It will be obvious," replied Ruby. "They'll see the witch clothes and they'll see the magical accessories and they'll put two and two together. Magic witches. Three magic witches."

"It does sound like fun," said Hilary slowly.

"We'll make wands and tiaras," said Ruby. "And we'll put on lots of jewelry."

"And maybe instead of black robes we could wear silver ones," said Lacey. "Or we could each wear a different color."

"But we don't want to look too much like princesses," said Hilary.

"Let's go downstairs and tell my mom about our costumes," said Lacey.

The girls ran downstairs, where they found Mrs. Morris in front of her computer.

"Mom!" cried Lacey. "Guess what we're going to be for Halloween. Three magic witches."

Mrs. Morris removed her reading glasses. "*Magic* witches?"

"Yes," said Lacey. "Magic witches are, um, they're . . ."

"Sort of like witch princesses," said Ruby.

"Oh, I see."

"And we might need some help with our costumes," Lacey went on. "You know, from you and Dad and Min and Flora and Hilary's parents."

"I'm here to help," said Mrs. Morris. "Tell me what you want to look like and we'll see what we can do."

Lacey, Hilary, and Ruby described their costumes, and Mrs. Morris made a list of supplies to buy. Then the girls returned to Lacey's room.

"How many days now until Halloween?" asked Ruby as she plopped onto Lacey's bed.

"Seventeen," replied Lacey promptly. "I counted this morning."

Ruby, instead of sounding excited, gave forth a noisy sigh.

"What?" said Lacey.

"Oh, it's just that Flora and Olivia and Nikki said they might not go trick-or-treating this year. They said they think they might be too old."

Lacey frowned. "So?"

"So last year we all went trick-or-treating together. Well, not Nikki. She wasn't allowed to go. But she was *supposed* to. We had plans."

"Well, you have plans with *us* this year," said Lacey.

"Yeah. What about the costumes we *just* talked about?" said Hilary, who was now frowning, too. "*We're* going together. Three magic witches, hello?"

Ruby squirmed. "I know. But I was hoping the others would come with us. I mean, in whatever costumes they want to wear. I don't like that they think they're too old to go trick-or-treating. And did you notice that they didn't say *I'm* too old for it?"

"But you *aren't* too old," said Lacey at the same time that Hilary said, "Do you *want* to be too old?" And after a moment, Lacey added, "It sounds kind of like you'd rather go out with them than with us."

"No, no!" cried Ruby. "That isn't it at all. It's . . . it's hard to explain."

Ruby looked at her friends. Hilary was staring moodily out the window again. Lacey was picking at the corner of her pillowcase and her lower lip was trembling.

"Hey, just forget about it, okay?" said Ruby. "Seriously. Come on. Let's think about our costumes. Lacey, you be a silver witch, and Hilary, you be a pink witch, and I'll be a blue witch. That's a good color combination. Now . . . what should we wear in our hair?"

CHAPTER 6

Patient Paw-Paw

"*Oh, doggie mine, doggie-doggie mine,*" sang Mae Sherman. "*Oh, doggie-doggie mine! I love you, doggie. I love you, love you, doggie. I think you are quite fine.*" She laid her cheek on Paw-Paw's soft head.

"Another good one," said Nikki, smiling at her sister.

It was a cool Saturday near the end of October, but sunny and so bright that Nikki, who was baby-sitting for Mae all day, had brought sunglasses outside for both of them. "What are some of the other dog songs you've written?"

"Well, my best one," replied Mae, puffing her chest out, "is the 'Supper Song.'"

"And how does that one go?" asked Nikki.

"Like this: *Supper for the pupper, supper for the pupper, supper for the pupperoo! Supper for my boy, supper for my boy, supper for me and you!*" Mae smiled, satisfied. "I love making up songs. You know what else is fun? Pretending Paw-Paw is in a fashion show, and then you get to say, '*Pre*-senting . . . Mister . . . Paw-Paw . . . Sherman!' And then it's like he just walked out on a stage in a gold suit and everyone is clapping for him." She smiled again. "Dogs sure are fun."

Mae, wearing the pink star-shaped sunglasses her big sister had handed her, sat contentedly on the front stoop. Nikki was next to her, and when she stretched her legs out straight, Mae stretched hers, too.

Mae decided there was nothing better than this fine Saturday, a day spent with her dog and her sister. She was in second grade this year, and so far, things were going well, even though Nikki no longer rode the bus with her. That was the only bad part about school days. Mae missed Nikki, plus there was no one to protect her from rude comments about her clothes and appearance. Nikki and their mother tried hard to keep up with the mending, and Mrs. Sherman did earn more money now than before, so the Shermans were able to buy new clothes and things more often. But Mae was still apt to climb aboard the school bus with holes in her sneakers or a tear in her backpack, out of which leaked work sheets and crayons. And then her fellow passengers might tweak papers from the backpack or snicker at her. Nine days earlier, an annoying third-grader had called out, "Nice shoes!" as Mae walked by in her holey sneakers. Quick as a flash, Mae plopped down next to her, squashing the third-grader's science project, which had been taking up half the seat. Then

Mae had leaned over and whispered loudly, "Do that again and I'll sit on something else. Go ahead — tell the bus driver. I don't care. Because then *I'll* tell him everything." She paused. "And he'll believe me."

Nothing further had been said to Mae (the driver hadn't been involved, either) so now even the bus rides weren't too bad. And then there was Miss Drew. Mae loved her teacher. She loved second grade, she loved reading, she loved library time and art time, but she especially loved Miss Drew, who lent her extra books to take home and was always willing to listen to a new dog song.

And now it was Saturday, and Mae had an entire day to spend with Nikki. Even her father wasn't around to spoil things. What could be better?

"Nikki? How come Mommy is working today?" Mae asked.

"You know she sometimes has to work on Saturday."

"But why?"

"She has a very big job at Three Oaks."

"Three Oaks is where the old people live."

Nikki nodded.

"Do we know anybody there?"

"Anybody who lives there? Well, I do, but I don't think you know them."

"Who?"

"Mr. and Mrs. Willet, who used to live in the Row Houses with Flora and Ruby and Olivia."

"Nope," said Mae. "Don't know them."

Nikki smiled. The previous Christmas, Mr. Willet had played Santa Claus and had visited the Shermans' house in his red suit and white beard. Mae had sincerely believed he was the real Santa.

"Well, they're very nice," said Nikki now. "But Mrs. Willet is having some trouble with her memory and she needs extra care, so Mr. Willet decided they should move to Three Oaks."

"Oh. Nikki?"

"Yeah?"

"So why is Mommy working today?"

"It's just part of her job. She runs the dining room there. And the dining room is very, very big. Even bigger than your school cafeteria. She has to arrange seating, and she oversees the staff — all the waiters and everyone. And today I think they're having a special event, which Mom is in charge of."

"Is she like a general?"

"More like a boss."

"Mommy is a boss?"

"Yup. But she has a boss, too."

"When I grow up, I'm going to be a veterinarian or else a queen."

"How about a songwriter?"

"I could be a queen *and* a songwriter."

"You could be a vet and a songwriter, too. I think you have a better shot at being a vet than a queen, by the way."

"Miss Drew says we can be anything we want. We just have to work for it."

"Yes, well . . . you do know that there are some things you really can't be, don't you?"

Mae frowned. "Like what?"

"Like a king."

"Why can't I be a king?"

"Because you aren't a boy."

"That's why I'm going to be a queen!" Mae exclaimed, exasperated.

Nikki sensed trouble. "You know what we should do today?" she said quickly.

"What," Mae replied flatly, staring at the dirt beneath her feet.

"Make Paw-Paw's costume for the dog parade. The parade is on Friday. That's in less than a week."

Mae gasped. "Really?"

"Yup. So have you been thinking about his costume?"

"Yes, but I can't decide on one."

"What are your choices?"

"Is it all up to me?"

"Within reason."

"What does that mean?"

"It means, I don't care what the costume is as long as we can actually make it. Don't choose something that's not possible."

"Miss Drew says anything is possible."

Nikki heaved a sigh. "Look, it has to be within our

means. We have to be able to make it or buy the supplies for it in six days, understood? And I don't have a lot of money, plus today Mom's not here, so we can't go into town to buy anything, anyway."

Mae nodded. "Okay. Well, I want Paw-Paw to be a princess."

"No kidding? Wouldn't it be more fun to dress him as, oh, a prince?"

"Miss Drew says —"

"Okay, okay. A princess. That's one good suggestion. What are the others?"

"I have to remember." Mae smoothed the fur on Paw-Paw's neck and said, "Wouldn't it be great if Paw-Paw had a mane? Then we could braid it."

Nikki didn't answer, fearing Mae would want to dress Paw-Paw as a horse, which she thought would be difficult.

"Well, how about a ghost?" Mae suggested after a moment. "That was one idea."

"Hmm. A ghost. All right. Let me start making a list."

By the time Mae ran out of ideas, the list included princess, ghost, angel, doctor, waitress, pirate, unicorn, and lion.

"Which one is your favorite?" Nikki asked her little sister.

Mae shrugged. "Which one is yours?"

Nikki carefully chose the one she thought would be the most difficult to make. "Lion," she replied.

"Okay. Let's make him a pirate."

"Good choice! All right. What does a pirate need?"

"An eye patch," Mae replied instantly. "A belt with a sword. Black clothes, I think. Some big jewelry. A bag of doubloons. Red-and-white-striped stockings. Oh, oh! And a parrot to sit on his shoulder, and we can use my stuffed parrot! We'll stick it to his shirt. And could we fasten a tape recorder to him?"

"Excuse me?" said Nikki. "A tape recorder?"

"So he can go 'Arghh, matey' as he walks along. We'll tape me saying it. Plus some other pirate things, like 'Walk the plank!' "

"Well." Nikki cleared her throat. "Let's start with the clothes. How are we going to get pants on him?" She eyed Paw-Paw, who was now looking at her nervously, as if he had just realized what was in store for him. His eyes had grown huge, and he was backing away slowly.

"Hmm," said Mae. "Maybe we could use a pair of my pajama bottoms. I don't have any black ones, but I guess that's okay. We could cut a hole in the back for his tail and just kind of slide them up and over his rump and then pull the drawstring around his waist. Do you think that would work?"

"Maybe," replied Nikki dubiously.

The girls set to work. They found a belt for Paw-Paw's middle and attached a bag to it labeled PIRATE'S TREASURE. (They filled the bag with pebbles.) They found an old pair of red-and-white-striped tights belonging to Mae. They were working on a pirate hat when Mae glanced down their lane and announced, "Mail's here! Let's go get the mail."

So they walked down the lane with Paw-Paw, and Mae proudly withdrew a handful of envelopes from the box. "Maybe there's a letter from Tobias," she said hopefully.

There wasn't. But there was an envelope with a return address Nikki recognized. "Oh, no," she said.

"What is it?" asked Mae.

"Something from Dad."

Mae said nothing.

Nikki studied the envelope and said, "It's addressed to The Shermans, so I guess I can open it. We don't have to wait for Mom." She slit the flap with her fingernail.

"Hey! Money!" said Mae, eyes wide, as she looked at the fistful of bills Nikki withdrew.

"Yeah," said Nikki.

"What's the matter? It's *money*. Isn't that good?"

"I guess. And there's no letter. That's even better."

"Come *on*," said Mae. "This is supposed to be a happy day. Hey, I know! We can make Paw-Paw's sword out of tinfoil. This is going to be so cool."

"Good idea," said Nikki, but Mae saw that her sister's eyes weren't smiling.

CHAPTER 7

New Neighbors at Last

The clanking that awakened Flora Northrop on the Saturday before Halloween sounded unlike the clanking of the highly annoying garbage trucks that rattled down Aiken Avenue very early in the morning. Flora sat up and scratched her head. Why did garbage trucks have to come around so *early*? she asked herself crabbily. Then she remembered that this was Saturday and the garbage trucks didn't come on Saturday, and anyway, as she had noted even in her sleep, the clanking somehow didn't sound like garbage-truck clanking.

Clank, she heard from below. Then *crash*.

Nope. Definitely not a garbage truck.

"Yo! Careful! Watch the side, watch the side, watch the *side!*"

"What on earth?" said Flora aloud, realizing that she sounded exactly like Min.

She got out of bed, raised her blinds, and peered out the window. In the street below, parked in front of the Willets' house, was a moving van so enormous that it was also parked in front of the Morrises' house and the Malones'.

Two muscular men had opened the back of the truck, which, fortunately for Flora, was facing in her direction so that she had a view of its contents. The men had set up a metal ramp leading from the open doors to the street several feet below. This, Flora thought, accounted for the clanking she had heard. The men were now hauling a couch down the ramp, the back of it apparently too close to the door frame. One of the men continued to shout, "Watch the side!"

"O-*kay!*" the other one exclaimed. "O-*kay!*"

Flora dashed to her door, across the hallway, and into Ruby's room. "Get up! Get up!" she said, shaking her sister's shoulder.

Ruby was sprawled in a tangle consisting not only of her bedclothes but also of the costume she had worn to her last dance class, the outfits she had worn to school the past three days, and a raincoat. King Comma emerged from under the tutu and mewed.

"You're waking up King Comma," muttered Ruby.

"I'm trying to wake up *you*," said Flora.

"It's Saturday." Ruby tucked her head under the pillow.

"I know. But I think you'll be interested to know that our new neighbors have arrived."

"I can't hear you," mumbled Ruby.

Flora lifted a corner of the pillow. "The new neighbors are here!" she said loudly.

Ruby sat up. "What? Really?"

"Yes! Come on!"

Flora and Ruby dressed in a flash.

"What time is it, anyway?" called Ruby, who was hopping on one foot, putting on her sock, and looking for her watch at the same time.

"Seven-thirty!" Flora called back.

"Is Min even up yet?"

"I don't know. Does it matter? Come *on!*"

Flora and Ruby clattered down the stairs, calling good morning to Min, who, it turned out, was in the kitchen, making coffee.

"Where are you going?" Min called back.

"To watch the new people move in. Their van's here!" said Flora.

"Find out their names," said Min. "They might not want to be referred to as 'the new people.'"

"Okay!" said Flora.

"Bye!" said Ruby.

"Take Daisy with you. She needs to go out!" called Min, but the door had already slammed behind her granddaughters.

Flora and Ruby stood on their stoop and tried to see into the depths of the van.

"Mattresses," said Ruby.

"A ton of boxes," said Flora.

"I don't see anything interesting."

"Like what?"

"Oh," said Ruby, "you know, a unicycle or a trampoline. Or a crystal ball!"

"Excuse me?" said Flora.

"A crystal ball. They could be wizards."

"I thought you wanted sextuplets."

"Wizards would be even better."

The girls stared at the van a few moments longer.

"I don't see any people," said Ruby eventually. "I mean, only the movers. Where's the family?"

"I don't know. Gosh, I bet Olivia would like to know what's going on. Do you think it's too early to ring her doorbell?"

"Let's throw pebbles at her window," said Ruby.

But that wasn't necessary. Olivia appeared on her front stoop, barefoot, wearing a flannel bathrobe.

"They're here!" Flora called.

"I know!"

"Well, come over so we can watch together."

"Like *this*?" cried Olivia.

"Of course not. Go get dressed."

"But hurry!" said Ruby.

Ten minutes later, Olivia had joined Flora and Ruby. The girls sat in a line on the stoop and watched the movers.

"I see a pink armchair," said Ruby. "That's nice. It must be for a girl."

"It could be for a living room," said Olivia.

"Or for a guy who likes pink," said Flora.

"There's a dresser," Ruby went on. "That must be for a boy. It's blue and it has baseballs and airplanes on it."

"A girl can't like baseballs and airplanes?" asked Flora.

"Oh, come on. I'm trying to figure out who's moving in. I'm trying to make obvious guesses."

"It's interesting to see what *isn't* in the van," remarked Olivia.

"What do you mean?" said Ruby.

"Well, no baby furniture."

"And no six of anything, so no sixtuplets," said Ruby. "Darn."

"I don't see any wizard equipment, either," said Flora, and Ruby poked her.

"Hey, now that some of the furniture's been taken off the truck, I can see what's written on the boxes," said Olivia, squinting. "Dishes."

"Boring," said Ruby.

"Linens."

"Boring."

"Winter coats."

"Boring."

Flora took her eyes from the van long enough to look up and down the street. From other stoops, from shadowed porches, through curtained windows, the people of Aiken Avenue kept watch on the second Row House from the left.

"When are the people going to get here?" asked Ruby finally. "I'm tired of guessing about them. I want to see them."

And at that very moment, a car drove slowly down Aiken and parked behind the van, leaving just enough room for the movers to continue their work.

Flora nudged Olivia and Ruby. "That must be them," she whispered.

The girls watched as all four doors of the car opened and out stepped a man, a woman, a girl about Flora's age, a boy of seven or eight, and . . .

"A dog!" exclaimed Olivia. "They have a dog." She paused. "I want a dog."

"We know," said Flora.

"Now Daisy Dear will have more dog company," said Ruby, staring. "Gosh, it's kind of a funny dog. It looks like a black-and-white Lab on dachshund legs."

The people who had been in the car now stood on the sidewalk and stretched. The girl reached back inside for a leash, which she clipped onto the dog's collar. The man spoke with the movers. (Flora tried to hear what they were saying, but she was too far away.) The woman gazed back and forth between the van and the Willets' front door. She tapped her chin with the palm of her hand. She walked three steps along the Willets' front walk, then three steps back, three steps forward, three steps back.

"What's she doing?" hissed Ruby.

"Gosh, I don't *know*," replied Flora, mystified.

Ruby's eyes widened. "Maybe they *are* wizards."

"Oh, they are not," said Olivia.

The girl bent over and spoke to the boy and they headed down Aiken, the dog jauntily leading the way.

"Let's go say hi," said Olivia. "Should we?"

"Okay," said Flora, but she suddenly felt shy.

Ruby was already running to the sidewalk. "Hi!" she called.

The girl and the boy turned toward her. "Hi," the girl replied cautiously.

Behind Flora, Min opened the door of the Row House long enough to let Daisy out. "Keep an eye on her," she called to Flora. "I have to get ready to go to the store."

In a flash, Daisy made a joyful beeline for the new dog, who reacted by leaping into the arms of the girl and yipping shrilly.

"Sorry! I'm sorry!" cried Flora.

"It's okay. Bessie's a big scaredy-cat," said the girl. Daisy stood on her hind legs, sniffing excitedly.

"So," said Ruby finally. "You're the new peo — I mean, you're moving into the Willets' — um . . ."

"What she means," said Flora, "is that you must be our new neighbors, and we're really glad you're moving in. I'm Flora and this is my sister, Ruby. We live here." She pointed over her shoulder. "And this is Olivia. She lives right there."

The girl smiled. "My name is Willow, and this is my brother, Cole."

Cole waved solemnly but said nothing.

"You're going to like it here," Olivia said to Cole. "There are a whole bunch of boys your age in the Row Houses."

"Is that what these houses are called?" said Willow. "The Row Houses?"

Olivia nodded.

"Are there really a lot of boys here?" asked Cole in a whisper.

"Four," Ruby told him. "Two down there at the end, next to you. That's the Morrises' house. And Olivia has two brothers."

Flora realized that Willow was still holding Bessie in her arms. "Here," she said, corralling Daisy. "Let me take her back inside. This is Daisy, by the way. Do you guys have to help your parents or can you stay here for a while?"

"My brothers will be out in a minute," added Olivia, turning to Cole. "You could meet them."

"I think we can stay," replied Willow, "but I'd better tell Mom what we're doing."

Five minutes later, Willow, free of Bessie (who had been taken to her new backyard), was sitting on the stoop with Flora, Olivia, and Ruby. Cole was standing in the yard next door with Henry, Jack, Travis, and Mathias.

"So where did you move from?" Ruby asked Willow. She glanced at Flora. "If that isn't too nosy."

Willow smiled. "It isn't nosy. We lived in New Hampshire. And we moved because my dad's job changed. It happened kind of suddenly. My mom, um, doesn't work," she added.

Flora regarded Willow, who actually looked, she decided, something like a willow tree. She was tall — taller than Flora — and slender with long hair that rippled down her back.

"What grade are you in?" asked Olivia.

"Seventh. I'll be going to . . ." Willow paused. " . . . to Camden Falls Central High School?"

"That's where we go!" said Flora. "I mean, where Olivia and I go. We're in seventh grade, too. Ruby's in fifth. She goes to the elementary school."

"I guess that's where Cole will go. He's in third grade."

"You can walk to school with us on Monday," offered Olivia.

"And when we get there, you can meet our other friend, Nikki," said Flora. "She doesn't live in the Row Houses."

"Thanks," said Willow. "What's the central high school like? Is it really a high school?"

"Yes and no," replied Olivia. "It's for grades seven through twelve, but the seventh- and eighth-graders spend most of their time in a separate wing. We don't have classes with the high school kids. But we all use the same cafeteria and gym and stuff."

Willow nodded. Then she glanced at Flora's front door. "Does your grandmother live with you?" she asked.

Flora smiled. "We live with her."

There was a lot to tell Willow, and she had a lot of questions about Camden Falls and Main Street and the Row Houses. By lunchtime, Flora was hungry, and suddenly she got to her feet and said, "Hey! I have an idea. We should all walk into town and have lunch at College Pizza. Then Olivia and Ruby and I could show you Needle and Thread and Sincerely Yours —"

"Willow? Cole?"

At the sound of her mother's voice, Willow jumped. "Uh-oh," she said under her breath. She stood up as her mother crossed the Malones' yard.

"Okay, time to come inside," called Mrs. Hamilton.

Willow looked at Cole, who was chasing Henry Walter in a game of tag.

"Couldn't we come later? Mom, these are my new friends, Olivia, Flo —"

"Time for lunch!" Mrs. Hamilton said again, this time more firmly.

"Mom —"

Mrs. Hamilton marched into Olivia's yard. "Cole. Lunchtime!"

Cole hesitated.

Mrs. Hamilton grinned suddenly. "I'm Mary Poppins!" she exclaimed. "Spit-spot! Come along now!" Her smile faded and she added, "I mean it."

"Bye," said Willow as she and Cole followed their mother back to their new house.

"Whoa," said Ruby when the Hamiltons had disappeared. "That is the weirdest mom in the universe."

"Hey," said Flora. "Look. Mrs. Hamilton's in their house pulling all the shades down. It's the middle of the day. Why's she doing that?"

"It sort of feels like she wants to keep us out," said Olivia.

"Or keep her family in," replied Flora.

CHAPTER 8

The Invitation

Olivia and Flora stood uncertainly on the sidewalk outside Willow Hamilton's house.

"All the shades are still down," said Olivia in a low voice.

"They've been like that since Mrs. Hamilton pulled them down on Saturday," Flora whispered.

"Huh. Well, what do you think we should do? We told Willow we'd walk with her to school this morning. But if we wait any longer, we'll be late."

"We can't leave without her. It's her first day."

"I guess we should go ring the bell," said Olivia.

"I guess."

The girls remained rooted to the sidewalk.

"I say we just leave," Olivia said finally. "We'll tell Willow —"

"Girls! Oh, girls!" Mrs. Hamilton opened the front door and waved to Olivia and Flora with a white handkerchief, as if she were at the prow of a steamer. "Are you the girls who are going to walk to school with my daughter? Well, never fear, Willow's here!"

Mrs. Hamilton stepped aside, and Willow emerged. She paused long enough to give her mother a brief hug, then ran to the sidewalk. "Hi!" she said. "Thank you for waiting."

Olivia glanced over her shoulder and saw Mrs. Hamilton tap several times on a large blue-and-white vase as she stepped inside the house. Then she touched her palm to her chin. "Willow," said Olivia, "is your mother —"

"I'm really glad you waited," said Willow in a rush. "*Really* glad. I wouldn't have wanted to go to school all by myself on the first day."

"Now Olivia and I can show you all the things we wanted to show you on Saturday," Flora said. "We'll walk right through town."

By the time Olivia, Flora, and Willow reached Central, Willow had heard about Mary Woolsey, who worked in Needle and Thread, and Sonny Sutphin, who had a job in Time and Again, and crabby Mrs. Grindle, who ran Stuff 'n' Nonsense. She had seen most of the stores and businesses on Main Street and knew that she wanted to try a scoop of Mr. Peanut ice cream at Dutch Haus.

Olivia thought Willow was nice, although Mr.

Peanut was fifth on the list of ice cream flavors she wanted to try. She was about to say so when Flora announced, "Nikki's bus is here."

Nikki and Willow were introduced then, the girls hurried inside, and before Olivia knew it, the day was half over and it was time for lunch.

"We should ask Willow to sit at our table," Olivia said as she stood behind Flora and Nikki in line in the cafeteria. But the girls couldn't find her.

"Was she in any of your classes?" asked Flora.

"Nope," said Olivia and Nikki. "Yours?"

"Just first period. I haven't seen her since then."

"Well, come on," said Olivia. "Maybe she'll find us."

They paid for their lunches and Olivia led the way to the table where they now regularly ate with Claudette Tisch, Mary Louise Detwiler, and Jacob, along with several others, kids who came and went. On the way, she squeezed by a table so crowded that extra chairs had been pulled up to it and even so, those chairs were filled and more kids were standing behind them, everyone talking and laughing. Olivia noted with a sense of mean pleasure that while Melody and Tanya were part of the group, eating sandwiches and calling merrily to someone across the table, they were among the kids standing up, the ones for whom chairs were not reserved, no longer the center of attention. And, Olivia thought, they looked as if they were working very hard to put on a show of having fun, a great deal of fun.

"Hey!" called Jacob as Olivia, Flora, and Nikki finally reached their own table. Olivia slid into the empty seat next to Jacob, the seat she suspected he had been saving for her.

Olivia smiled. "Hi." She looked at the array of food on her tray and raised a tuna sandwich to her mouth. She lowered it. Jacob's eyes were on her. "What?" she said, turning to him.

Jacob's pale face suddenly burned a bright red, a flush that began at his neck and crept upward. "Um, nothing."

Olivia returned to her sandwich. She could still feel Jacob watching her, a physical sensation as real as if he had tapped her on the shoulder. *"What?"* she said again, replacing the sandwich on her plate.

Jacob opened his mouth, closed it, then opened it and said, "Could I talk to you for a minute?"

"Sure."

"I mean in private."

"Oh." Olivia could think of nothing further to say.

Jacob got to his feet. He looked around the packed cafeteria. "Come on."

Olivia glanced at Nikki and Flora, shrugged, abandoned her lunch, and followed Jacob to a corner of the room where miraculously one entire table was empty. She started to sit down but saw that Jacob was leaning against the wall, so she leaned against it, too, palms flat behind her, trying to appear nonchalant. "Jacob?" she said.

"Um, yes. Well."

Olivia hesitated. "Did you want to ask me something?" Her palms were growing sweaty against the wall.

"Yes." Jacob was then silent for so long that Olivia looked in desperation across the room to her table, where, she now saw, Nikki and Flora were craning their necks, trying to get a good view of her and Jacob.

"Jacob?"

"Okay. Here's the thing," he said at last. "I was wondering if you wanted to go to the Halloween dance with me. If you don't want to," he rushed on, "it's okay. I understand. But I'd really like to go with you. I mean, I'd like you to go with me. Or for us to go together. Whatever. So will you? I mean, will you come with me?"

Olivia's mouth had parted slightly and she found herself unable either to close it or to open it the rest of the way. Was Jacob asking her on a date? Did a dance count as a date? Well, of course it did, she told herself. Why wouldn't a dance count as a date? Then another thought occurred to her: Should she consult with Flora and Nikki before giving Jacob an answer? For that matter, should she ask her parents for permission?

Next to her, Jacob slumped against the wall. "Like I said, if you don't want to go —"

"No!" exclaimed Olivia, recovering. "No, it isn't that I don't want to go." She paused, realizing that she had to give Jacob an answer. "I do want to go," she said. "I mean, yes, I'll go to the dance with you."

"You *will*?"

Olivia nodded. "Yes. Thank you."

"You're welcome."

Olivia had the feeling that Jacob wanted to jump up and down and shout "Wah-hoo!" — which is exactly what she wanted to do. Instead, he pushed himself away from the wall and strode back to their table.

Olivia followed him. Nikki's and Flora's eyes were boring into her as she approached their table, but they had the good sense not to ask what had happened. Which meant that they had to wait until after school to get the story.

The second they met at Olivia's locker, Nikki said, "Okay. Tell us right now! We can't wait a moment longer."

"Jacob asked me to go to the Halloween dance with him."

"No!" Nikki punched Olivia in the arm. "For real?"

Olivia grinned. "Yup."

"Hey, that's . . . that's great," said Flora quietly.

"Yeah, it really is!" exclaimed Nikki.

Olivia bounced through the hallways, followed by a jubilant Nikki and a somewhat plodding Flora.

"Do you think we should wait for Willow?" asked Flora as they approached the door.

"Did you guys make plans with her?" said Nikki.

"Not really."

"Then let's just go. I want to hear more about Jacob."

"You're coming with us?" Flora asked Nikki.

"Yup. Mom can pick me up later."

"There really isn't anything else to tell," said Olivia as they crossed the lawn and headed for Main Street. "I mean, that was it. Jacob just asked me if I'd go with him."

"And you said yes."

Olivia nodded. "Hey!" she exclaimed suddenly, looking alarmed. "You guys are going to go to the dance, too, aren't you? I don't want to go without you."

"Of course we're going," replied Nikki.

"Wow. That means no trick-or-treating," said Flora.

"I thought you didn't want to go trick-or-treating," said Olivia.

"I hadn't one hundred percent made up my mind. It's a little sad to think that last year was our last year of trick-or-treating on Main Street."

"It doesn't have to be your last year *ever*," said Nikki. "Look at all the adults who still go."

"But it isn't the same. You know it isn't."

"Well, gosh, if you guys don't go to the dance —" Olivia started to say.

"I didn't say we weren't going to go. I just said not trick-or-treating would be sad." Flora kicked at a pebble.

Olivia stepped on it. "Somehow I thought you'd be more excited about my news."

Flora shook her head. "It's funny. The other thing I kind of wanted to do on Halloween was to stay at home and hand out candy. It seemed so grown-up. Why can't I make up my mind?"

Olivia felt like saying, "Why can't you just be happy for me?" but she had the sense to say nothing at all.

"Just out of curiosity, why do you want Nikki and me to go to the dance with you?"

"Are you kidding?!" exclaimed Olivia. "Why do I want you to *go*? I want you to go because even with Jacob I'm going to be a target for Melody and Tanya. Like a great big bull's-eye. There might as well be an arrow pointing to my head, too. And a sign reading KICK ME."

"Okay, okay," said Flora.

"So you want us to be, like, your bodyguards?" asked Nikki.

Olivia laughed. "Not exactly. I just want you to be there."

"It's going to be fun," said Nikki.

Flora remembered her excitement when she had first seen the sign announcing the dance. "It *is* going to be fun," she said at last. And she set aside the unsettling thought that she was jealous because Olivia had a date.

CHAPTER 9

Something Strange

There was something strange about the Hamiltons. No, not about all the Hamiltons, Flora corrected herself. Just about Mrs. Hamilton. There was definitely something strange, very strange, about Mrs. Hamilton.

Willow was nice. And Cole was nice, although he was shy, but Flora certainly couldn't fault anyone for being shy. Mr. Hamilton seemed nice enough, too, but busy at his job, so Flora hadn't seen him more than two or three times. Mrs. Hamilton, on the other hand . . .

"Goodness me," said Min on Monday evening when Flora told her how Willow's mother had stood at the front door and waved to her and Olivia with a handkerchief. "Although really, when you think about it — waving with a hankie. It isn't as though she was running up and down Aiken Avenue in a gorilla suit."

"No," said Flora slowly.

"Still," said Ruby.

"What is it, girls?" asked Min.

Ruby shrugged. "It's hard to explain. She laughs when you wouldn't expect her to."

"And she makes jokes that only she thinks are funny," said Flora. "I feel a little creepy when I'm around her."

"It's hard to explain," said Ruby again.

"Maybe she's shy," suggested Min.

"Maybe," Flora agreed. "Cole's shy."

Flora, Ruby, and Min were sitting at the kitchen table, eating a late supper. A silence followed Flora's last comment that was so long that Ruby deliberately broke it with a harsh belch that startled Daisy Dear and caused her to go skidding out of the kitchen.

"Ruby!" exclaimed Min.

"I thought we needed a little comedy relief."

"Comic relief," Min corrected her. "Maybe we do."

Min looked troubled. Flora saw an expression on her face that she saw again the next day on Mrs. Morris's face when Travis, trying bravely not to cry, came home complaining that Cole's mother had scared him when he and Cole were playing hide-and-seek.

"What did she do?" asked Mrs. Morris.

"She jumped out of a closet and shouted BOO!"

Flora almost laughed, then realized how troubled she would have been if an adult — one she didn't know well — had done that to her at Travis's age.

Mrs. Morris frowned at the house next door before leading Travis inside, her arm around his shoulders.

Early on Wednesday morning — so early that the streetlights were still ablaze — the telephone rang at Flora's house. She heard it faintly, ringing twice in Min's room before it stopped. Flora could imagine her grandmother answering it sleepily but trying to sound alert. A phone call at that hour couldn't be good news, thought Flora. But when a few minutes passed and she heard nothing further from Min's room, she decided it had been a wrong number and fell soundly asleep, waking again only when her alarm went off.

"Who called?" was the first thing Ruby said at the breakfast table that morning.

"Good morning, Min dear," was Min's reply.

"Good morning, Min dear," said Ruby obediently. Then she added, "Good morning, Flora dear. Good morning, King Comma dear. Good morning, Daisy Dear dear." She looked quite satisfied with herself.

"Lord above," murmured Min.

"So who called?" asked Ruby. "I heard the phone ring at, like, three o'clock."

"Well, it was five o'clock," replied Min. "But still." She hesitated, spending a long time buttering a piece of toast. "The caller was Mrs. Hamilton," she said finally.

"What was wrong?" asked Flora. "Are they okay?"

"They're fine." Min frowned. "I don't think Mrs. Hamilton had any idea what time it was. She said she was calling to thank me for the cake I brought over on Sunday."

"She was thanking you at five in the morning?" said Ruby.

"I know." Min shook her head. "She sounded awfully confused. Or nervous. It was hard to tell. Then she started talking about a particular kind of cake her mother used to make, and then she wanted to know what grocery store we go to. I was about to ask her if we could talk later in the morning when she suddenly said she had to hang up — and she did. Hang up, I mean."

"Huh," said Flora.

"Wacko," said Ruby.

"Ruby," said Min.

"Sorry," said Ruby. She leaned under the table to sneak a bite of toast to Daisy. "But she is," she muttered.

That afternoon, a gray day that felt more like November than October, Flora walked home from school with Willow. Above them, seven geese honked noisily as they flew over Main Street.

Willow shivered and fastened the top button on her coat. She glanced up. "Those geese are lazy," she said. "They didn't even bother to make a V. It's more like an L." She paused to read a sign in the window of Time and Again. "Dog parade? What's a dog parade?" she asked.

Flora smiled. "That was Nikki's idea. It's a Halloween parade for dogs. It's a fund-raiser for the animal shelter. Hey! You guys should enter Bessie. There's still time."

"Maybe," said Willow. "So let me get this straight. Your grandmother and Olivia's grandmother own the sewing store, right?"

"Right," said Flora.

"And Olivia's parents own — what's it called? Yours Truly?"

"Sincerely Yours. It's right back there. Olivia's helping out this afternoon. That's why she didn't walk home with us."

The girls turned the corner onto Dodds Lane.

"Anyway, we're entering Daisy in the parade," said Flora. "Ruby and I. We're going to dress her as a daisy."

"Did you know that Cole does sixth-grade math and he's only in third grade?"

"I — well, no, I didn't know that." Flora eyed Willow.

"Yup. He's really amazing. Is this where we turn?"

Flora nodded. Ahead were the Row Houses. She liked this view of them, from back at the corner, where she could see the rows of everything — the sixteen third-floor windows, the sixteen second-floor windows, the eight front doors, the eight front stoops, the eight yards, one after another. She noticed now that the

Hamiltons' door was open and Willow's mother was standing on their stoop.

"Your mom's waiting," said Flora, glancing at Willow.

"Yeah."

"Does she always wait like that?"

Willow shrugged. "I never know what she's going to do. . . . Oh, well." They drew up to the Hamiltons' walk and Willow said, "I'll see you tomorrow."

"Oh," said Flora, who had been about to invite Willow to her house. "Okay. See you tomorrow." She edged down the sidewalk. When she reached the Malones' house, she turned around. Willow was approaching her mother, who stood like a grim statue before the front door, arms folded across her chest.

"So?" said Mrs. Hamilton.

"I . . . what?" replied Willow uncertainly.

Flora could hear their voices perfectly. She bent and pretended to re-tie her sneaker.

"You know what," said Mrs. Hamilton.

"I really don't. Um, my shoes?"

"No, not your shoes! Your closet door. How many times do I have to remind you? Can't you remember a single thing?"

Flora risked a glance over her shoulder. Willow had backed down a step. "I promise I'll do it right," she said. "I'll do it this minute." She hesitated. "Can I come inside?"

Mrs. Hamilton stared at her. "Fine." Then, "*Fine.*" She jerked Willow's elbow as Willow squeezed by her. Then she slammed the door closed with such force that Flora heard windows rattle.

On Wednesday afternoon, Ruby and Olivia had after-school activities, so Flora sat on her stoop, presiding over the younger Row House children: the Morrises, Olivia's brothers, and Cole Hamilton. She wasn't officially baby-sitting, but she liked to give the appearance of a baby-sitter, figuring it was good advertising.

Presently, Mrs. Hamilton called to Cole and handed him a leash, Bessie on the other end of it. "Bessie needs to get out for a while," she said.

Flora watched Cole run along the sidewalk with Bessie. "Hey, Cole!" she called. "Did Willow tell you about the dog parade?"

Cole came to a stop, turned, and walked Bessie across Flora's lawn. "What dog parade?"

"It's on Friday afternoon." Flora once again described Nikki's idea. "It should be a lot of fun," she added. "And I could help you with a costume. There's still time, if we pick something simple. I could make Bessie into —"

But Cole was shaking his head. "No."

"There's time, Cole. Really," said Flora. "And, hey! On Saturday, you could take Bessie trick-or-treating with you! She'd have her very own costume. Wouldn't that be fun? I bet Bessie hasn't been trick-or-treating before."

"Okay . . ." said Cole. He paused. "Well, actually, no."

"But why not?"

"There's no point. My mom won't let me go to the parade without an adult."

"Well, couldn't you go with the Morrises? Or how about with Willow? Or with your own mom? Why doesn't she take you?"

Cole shook his head again. "She won't."

"She won't let you go without an adult or with an adult? That doesn't seem fair. Look, I'm really good at sewing. I could whip up a costume for Bessie in no time. Let's go talk to your mother." Flora took Cole by the hand and led him and Bessie back to his house.

"Flora, no. This isn't going to work."

"Oh, come on."

"Really. My mom doesn't —"

Flora had reached the Hamiltons' stoop. She knocked on the door, and when Mrs. Hamilton opened it, she told her about the parade. "And I could help Cole with the costume," she said finally, then stopped talking when she realized with astonishment that Mrs. Hamilton was starting to cry. And not in that silent way in which Min occasionally cried. No, after just a few moments, she was wailing with full force like a child about to have a temper tantrum.

Mrs. Hamilton drew in a shaking breath, then let out a loud, long sob. "No! I won't have Cole going to such a crowded event."

Flora took a step backward.

"I won't!" cried Mrs. Hamilton. She pulled Cole and Bessie through the front door and shut it hastily.

Flora stood for a moment before the house with its shades drawn. Then she turned and ran all the way to Main Street and the safety of Needle and Thread.

CHAPTER 10

Dogs on Parade

Paw-Paw Sherman sat drooling in the backseat of the car, watching the county road speed by. Nikki wondered what else he saw, what dogs truly saw when they stared so intently out a car window.

"I think he looks handsome, don't you?" said Mae to the passengers in the car.

"He's the best pirate dog I've ever seen," replied Mr. Pennington seriously.

"Thank you very much for bringing us into town," said Nikki. "We really appreciate it."

"Well, we can't have the person behind the parade miss it," said Mr. Pennington. "That would be a travesty. I was happy to pitch in when your mother called."

Nikki turned around. Behind her, Mae was strapped into a booster seat. On one side of her was Paw-Paw the pirate. On the other side was Jacques, wearing a sailor suit and trying to remove the hat.

"Excuse me, Mr. Pennington?" said Mae. "I don't think Jacques likes his costume."

Mr. Pennington smiled. "I don't think so, either. If he's fooling with the hat, you can take it off of him."

Nikki faced front again. They were nearing town, and as they passed a large Victorian house she saw a woman walk across the lawn, leading a small curly-haired dog in a red costume with a great number of appendages.

"Hey!" exclaimed Nikki, laughing. "That dog is dressed as a lobster!"

"I see a dog in a clown suit," said Mae.

And Mr. Pennington said, "My goodness. Look at Main Street. I'd better park here. I don't think we'll be able to get all the way into town."

Nikki squinted down the block. "Wow," she said under her breath. Then more loudly, "Wow!"

"And this was all your idea," said Mr. Pennington as he unloaded Jacques and Paw-Paw from the backseat.

"I never dreamed so many people would come," said Nikki, awestruck, as Mr. Pennington helped Mae climb out. "Never in a million years. This is amazing."

"Cool!" cried Mae. "I see the ice cream truck. Oh, and the balloon man and he's selling dog-shaped balloons! This is like a fair. Can I have a balloon, please? Can I?"

Nikki pulled Mae aside. "I have a little money from Mom," she told her quietly, "but remember that we're

Mr. Pennington's guests. Don't ask for a lot of stuff. He did us a big favor by driving us here. Come on. Concentrate on walking in the parade."

Mae pouted briefly but perked up when she spotted a young woman carrying a poodle dressed as a ballerina.

"Miss Drew!" exclaimed Mae rapturously. "It's Miss Drew! Hi, Miss Drew."

"Hello, Mae," said her teacher. "This is Buzzy. Is that Paw-Paw?"

Mae nodded. "And this is my sister, Nikki, and this is Mr. Pennington. Oh, and over there is Jacques. He's Mr. Pennington's dog. I didn't know you were going to be in the parade. Hey, did you know the parade was my sister's idea?"

"Was it?" said Miss Drew. "Well, it's a great idea."

"Thank you," replied Nikki. "It's to raise money for the animal shelter."

Miss Drew held out a red ticket. "I just paid my entrance fee. Buzzy and I are ready to march."

"We have to go pay our fees," said Nikki.

"I'll see you later, Miss Drew!" called Mae.

Nikki, Mae, and Mr. Pennington made their way through the crowd on Main Street.

"Where do we sign up?" asked Mr. Pennington. He tugged at Jacques's leash. "Come on, boy." Jacques had planted his feet firmly on the sidewalk and refused to move. Mr. Pennington sighed. "It's the costume. He really doesn't like to wear clothes. I hope he'll walk in the parade." He stooped to pick up the recalcitrant Jacques.

"The registration booth is over there," said Nikki, pointing to the town square. "I think Harriet is going to be collecting the money."

"Nikki!" called Mae as they stepped around costumed dogs and threaded their way through knots of people. "Paw-Paw's stockings are coming off!"

Nikki turned around and saw that Paw-Paw's red-and-white-striped pirate's stockings were pooling around his feet.

"And now he's stepping out of them!" exclaimed Mae. She gathered up the stockings and handed them to her sister.

Nikki sighed. "I'll try to get them back on him in just a minute. Let me pay the fee first."

Nikki and Mr. Pennington waited in line at the booth that had been set up in the square, while Mae sat nearby with Paw-Paw, who was now tugging at the bag attached to his belt.

"Hi, Harriet," Nikki said as she stepped up to the booth.

"Nikki! My goodness. Can you believe the number of people who are here? I've lost track of how many tickets we've sold, and the people with the collection canisters are doing well, too." Harriet peered behind Nikki. "Where's Paw-Paw?"

"On that bench with Mae. His costume is coming off. Harriet, this is Mr. Pennington."

Nikki and Mr. Pennington paid their registration fees, even though Harriet claimed that Nikki should be allowed to walk in the parade for free.

"Thank you," said Nikki, "but I want to contribute, too. I have my money right here."

Harriet grinned. "Well, we appreciate it. Believe me, every bit helps. When you get Paw-Paw's costume straightened out, go down the street to the community center. The parade will start there. You can see people lining up already. Hold on to your tickets. You'll have to turn them in before you can join the parade."

A few minutes later, Jacques, dragging his feet, and Paw-Paw, stockings bagging once more, allowed themselves to be led to the community center.

"Look, there are Flora and Ruby!" said Nikki as she and Mae and Mr. Pennington edged along the sidewalk. "Hi, Flora! Hi, Ruby!"

"Oh, Daisy is so *cute*!" cried Mae. "She's a . . . oh, I get it. She's a daisy."

"Great costume," said Nikki admiringly.

"Thank you," said Flora.

"Thank you," said Ruby.

Flora glared at Ruby. "You didn't have anything to do with the costume."

"I did too! I watched you cut out all those felt petal things and I kept saying, 'Nice job, Flora.'"

"Girls," said Mr. Pennington, "I see your aunt Allie. She's waving to you."

Flora and Ruby stood on their tiptoes and peered across the street. Sure enough, their aunt was smiling and waving. She held up a camera. "I'm going to take pictures!" she called. "I'll be standing in front of Needle and Thread with Min. Nikki, I'll take pictures of you and Mae and Paw-Paw, too."

"Oh, that'll be great," called Nikki. "Then Mom will be able to see the parade."

"Come on. Let's go hand in our tickets and get in line," said Ruby. "Maybe we'll be right up front where people can see us better. Hey, maybe we'll get our pictures in the paper."

"In the *paper*?!" said Mae, her voice rising to a squeak. "Oh, goody, goody. I want to be in the paper. I want to be famous."

"Oh, lord. Mae's going to be another Ruby," Flora whispered to Nikki.

They turned in their tickets and joined the line of people and dressed-up doggies. Once again, Jacques refused to move, and once again, Mr. Pennington picked him up. "But if you think I'm going to carry you all the way down Main Street," Mr. Pennington said to him, "you have another think coming."

"Oh! Oh, no!" exclaimed Flora suddenly. She started to laugh. "Look over there."

Joining the parade were Mr. and Mrs. Fong. They were pulling a wagon, and in the wagon were Grace and their two small dogs, all dressed as pigs. A sign on the wagon read THE THREE LITTLE PIGS.

"Ha!" cried Ruby. "That's a good one." She looked at her watch. "When's the parade supposed to start?" she asked.

"In ten minutes," Nikki replied.

"Not a moment too soon," said Mr. Pennington, looking around at dogs pulling their hats off, dogs lying down in the street, little dogs barking at big dogs, owners preventing fights, and everywhere discarded booties, socks, bandannas, tiaras, and angel wings.

At four o'clock exactly, a whistle blew. Before Nikki knew it, she was marching down Main Street, holding Mae with her left hand and Paw-Paw's leash with her right. Lining both sides of the street were people laughing and clapping and taking pictures. Behind her, Mr. Pennington walked with Jacques, who had deigned to follow him at an excruciatingly slow pace. Next to her were Flora, Ruby, and Daisy Dear. Daisy, Nikki thought, looked somewhat embarrassed. She plodded along, eyes focused straight ahead, and refused to turn her head, no matter how often Flora and Ruby called to her.

"Nikki! Flora! Ruby! Mr. Pennington!"

Nikki was aware of a small figure springing up and down, up and down in the crowd to her left. "Hi, Olivia!" she called.

"Look behind you!" Olivia called back.

Nikki turned around. She saw a Great Dane in a cowboy costume. She saw a police dog dressed as a police officer. She saw a stubborn bichon that had apparently discarded his entire costume, since he was wearing nothing at all and his owner was carrying an armful of tiny clothes. She saw a bulldog puppy dressed as a baby — a bonnet on her head, a pacifier on a string around her neck, booties on her feet — being carried down the street in the arms of a tall man. And then she realized who the man was.

"Mr. Barnes! Hi, Mr. Barnes!" she called to her English teacher.

"Hello, Nikki," he replied. "Hi, Flora." He waved the puppy's paw. "This is Shortbread. She's ten weeks old."

"Oh, she's so *cute!*" cried Mae.

Nikki, laughing, continued down the street. She waved to Sonny Sutphin in front of Time and Again, and he waved back. She waved to Aunt Allie, Min, Gigi, and Mary Woolsey in front of Needle and Thread, and Allie snapped photos of her and Mae and Paw-Paw, of Flora and Ruby and Daisy Dear, of Mr. Pennington and Jacques, and even of Mr. Barnes, whom Allie recognized as her neighbor. (Mr. Barnes held Shortbread on her back and pretended to give her a bottle.)

Three blocks down Main Street, the parade came to an end. Harriet found her and said, "Nikki, come here a minute." She tugged at Nikki's elbow, and Nikki, with Mae and Paw-Paw in tow, followed her back to College Pizza, where a reporter from the paper interviewed her about the parade.

"Me. She interviewed *me*," she said later to Flora and Ruby.

When the paper came out the following week, it featured a whole page of photos of the dog parade and a separate article about Nikki and Harriet and Sheltering Arms. Nikki's mother framed the article and hung it in the Shermans' living room.

CHAPTER 11

Aunt Allie's Mystery

Ruby walked home from the parade with Flora and Daisy Dear. Daisy was now naked. And the moment her costume had come off, her personality had returned.

"What *hap*pened to her when she was wearing the daisy?" Ruby asked her sister as they approached the Row Houses.

"I don't know," replied Flora. "It's a mystery. She wouldn't look at us, she wouldn't turn her head." Flora paused. "It was like she was embarrassed."

"I didn't know dogs could get embarrassed," said Ruby. "Try putting the daisy back on her."

Flora obligingly fastened the petal collar around Daisy's neck again, and Daisy came to a complete halt and stood motionless on the sidewalk, eyes straight ahead.

"Daisy!" said Ruby loudly.

"Daisy!" said Flora.

Daisy had turned to cement.

"Okay, take it off," said Ruby.

Flora removed it and Daisy sprang to life.

"Wow," exclaimed Ruby. "Wouldn't you like to know what's going on in her head?"

"Hey, Ruby!" Lacey Morris charged along the sidewalk from the direction of Main Street.

"Did you see us in the parade?" Ruby called to her.

"Yes. You were great. Ruby, we need to work on our costumes."

"I can't. I'm having a sleepover at my aunt's house tonight."

"But Halloween is tomorrow and the costumes aren't finished."

At this, Flora narrowed her eyes. "What do you mean, your costumes aren't finished? Lacey, your mom and Min and I did most of the work on them. All you guys were in charge of were the last few little things."

Ruby and Lacey glanced at each other and then down at the sidewalk.

"Ruby . . ." said Flora.

"We changed our minds," Ruby muttered.

"What?! You changed your *minds*? You mean, you're not going to be the Eiffel Tower, the Statue of Liberty, and the Leaning Tower of Pisa?" (Ruby and her friends had, in fact, changed their minds so often that Flora had never even heard about the three magic witches.)

"Actually," said Lacey, "she means we're not going to be the bouquet of flowers. We did change our minds about the Eiffel Tower and stuff" (Flora's mouth was hanging open), "so then we started work on this flower idea we'd had before, but we didn't finish that, either."

"And just when were you going to tell your mom and Min and me that you weren't going to wear the costumes we made you?"

"Tomorrow night?" said Lacey in a small voice.

"Well, that's nice." Flora shook her head. "All that work."

"Oh, come on, Flora. Don't be mad," said Ruby. "You made really, really great costumes. It's just that . . . there are so many things we could be. We really can't make up our minds. This isn't something to be taken lightly," she added primly.

"So now you need help finishing your flower costumes?" asked Flora.

"No, we don't need help," Lacey replied. "We just need time." She eyed Ruby.

"Well, I'm sorry!" exclaimed Ruby. "I'm going to my aunt's tonight. We can finish the costumes tomorrow. We have all day."

"I guess," said Lacey.

"I promise I'll come over as soon as I get home. I'll call Hilary then and tell her to come over, too."

"Okay. Hey! You know what we should be? A fork, a knife, and a spoon."

"Ooh, ooh! Or three *trolls*! Wouldn't that be cool?" cried Ruby.

Later, when Min was driving Ruby across Camden Falls to Allie's house, Ruby forgot about Halloween costumes and turned her attention to the reason for the sleepover. It was a reason of which her aunt was unaware.

Ruby could not forget the closetful of baby items she and Flora had found the month before. The closet and its contents were a mystery, and the mystery was begging to be solved. Ruby wished Flora could have come along to help her, but Flora, Olivia, and Nikki were having a pre-dance sleepover at Olivia's house.

So, it's all up to me, Ruby thought as Min pulled into Allie's driveway. And then she added, Think like a detective.

The front door of the house opened and Allie stepped out, waving. Min said, "Have fun. Call me in the morning."

"Okay," said Ruby. "Bye!" She ran inside. "Hi, Aunt Allie! I'm going to put my stuff in my room, okay?"

"Great. I'll be downstairs making dinner."

Perfect, thought Ruby. She hurried to the second floor and along the hall to the room that Allie had fixed up for Flora and Ruby. She had decorated it just for them when she had bought the house over the summer. Ruby dumped her duffel bag on one of the beds and sat on the other one to think.

You're a detective, she thought, and you're at the scene of a crime. Now, what should be your first move?

She fingered a china leopard while she thought. The answer came to her quickly. First she should examine the crime scene itself. That would be the closetful of baby things. Then she should look for clues.

But what kind of clues? Ruby thought some more. She needed to find out why the clothes were there and what they could mean. In order to do that, she needed to know more about her aunt Allie. And in order to do that, she should search . . . well, she should search the whole house, but she didn't have time for that. She was only there for one night. So she should start with the most obvious places. And those, she decided, would be Allie's study and Allie's bedroom.

"Ruby?" called her aunt from downstairs.

Ruby jumped guiltily to her feet and set the leopard back on its shelf. "Coming!"

"You don't have to come right this second," her aunt called back. "But dinner will be ready in ten minutes, okay?"

"Okay!"

Ten minutes. That was just enough time in which to survey the contents of the closet again.

Ruby crept down the hall. She stood before the closet door with her hand on the knob and then thought that perhaps she should have some sort of prop with her in case Aunt Allie suddenly came up the stairs. She tiptoed into the bathroom, pulled the towel off the rack, and carried it back out into the hall. If her aunt appeared, she would tell her she was looking for a larger bath towel and had opened the door to the wrong closet (which was pretty much how she and Flora had discovered the baby clothes in the first place).

Ruby, breathing heavily and listening for the sound of her aunt's footfalls, placed her hand on the knob of the door that she knew was not the linen closet. Slowly, she turned it, drawing in her breath at the sound of a soft click. She eased the door open. There before her were the shelves and shelves of baby things, many of them looking as though they might be for a girl, and all of them brand-new. Some of them were still in their plastic wrappers. Ruby took a step closer. She leaned forward to finger a package of yellow diaper covers. Each was decorated with a white duck. She saw a stack of clothes that were not in their wrappers and drew them forward.

A pink-and-purple-striped shirt with rosebuds around the collar.

A blue-and-white shirt. No, Ruby realized as she unfolded it. Not a shirt — a dress. A tiny dress.

Next to the stack of clothes was a pair of pale yellow shoes, each with a strap that fastened with a Velcro flower.

"Ruby? Dinner!" Aunt Allie's voice floated up the stairs.

Ruby jumped a mile and knocked a box to the floor of the closet. The box contained a baby monitor, and it hit the floor with a thud.

"Ruby?" her aunt called again. "Are you all right?"

Ruby hastily replaced the box and closed the door. "Yup!" she replied. "Be right there!"

Ruby's heart was pounding, but she was proud of herself. She had completed the first of her tasks, examining the scene of the crime. She knew that technically the closet was not the scene of any crime, but she didn't know what else to call it, and anyway, "scene of the crime" had a very exciting ring to it.

Ruby ate her entire dinner wondering how she could search Aunt Allie's study, and just as they were finishing their dessert (Ruby used the term loosely, since she herself did not consider sliced peaches a dessert), the telephone rang.

"Excuse me," said Aunt Allie. She answered the phone, listened for a moment, then said to Ruby, "Sorry, this is going to take a little while, but I'll try to keep it as short as possible. We can make popcorn when I finish, if you like."

"Oh!" Ruby brightened. "That's okay. Don't worry about the call. Um, take your time."

Ruby knew that a good niece would clean up the kitchen while her aunt was busy, but Ruby couldn't waste this opportunity. While Allie sat at the kitchen table, making notes on a pad of paper, Ruby slipped down the hall and stood at the entrance to the study. She glanced over her shoulder a couple of times, and when she could still hear her aunt talking on the phone, she stole into the room. One step, two, then three, then four and she had reached the desk. Gingerly, she slid out the chair and sat on it. She clasped her hands together, unclasped them, and at last she opened the top desk drawer, the long one above her knees.

Ruby, trying to listen for sounds from the kitchen and search for clues at the same time, saw several markers, a pile of rubber bands, a container of paper clips, a ruler, a stack of blank mailing labels, and a roll of return address labels.

"Well. This is dull," said Ruby aloud.

She closed the drawer, eyed the three stacked drawers to her left, and opened the top one. Here she found stationery and postcards. "Bor —" she started to say, but then she noticed other things. In one corner were two photos of her and Flora taken over the summer. She found a letter from Allie's editor. She found some business cards and a reminder to make an appointment to have her teeth cleaned at Dr. Malone's.

Ruby was about to close the drawer and tackle the one below when her eye fell on another photo. This one showed Aunt Allie posing with an incredibly handsome man in front of a building that Ruby guessed was somewhere in New York City. Both Allie and the man were grinning widely and her aunt was making the thumbs-up sign. Ruby turned the photo over. On the back a date had been scribbled — July of the summer before Allie had moved back to Camden Falls.

"Huh," said Ruby aloud. And then her eyes fell on a slender envelope. The return address was Guatemala. "Whoa," said Ruby. She reached for the envelope.

"Ahem."

Ruby jerked her hand back and slammed the drawer shut so quickly that she nearly caught her fingers in it. Her aunt was standing in the doorway.

"I — I was just looking for a pen," said Ruby, reddening, as she noticed a jar of pens sitting in plain view on top of the desk.

Her aunt looked away. "Well. Time for popcorn," she said.

Ruby stared. Didn't her aunt know she was lying about the pens? Wasn't she going to ask Ruby any questions?

Ruby grabbed a pen from the jar (she might as well follow through with her lie) and joined Allie in the kitchen.

All evening she waited for the questions to come but none did. It was as if, Ruby thought later as she lay in bed trying to fall asleep, her aunt didn't want to talk about what had happened. And that didn't make any sense to Ruby. Why didn't Allie want to talk about it?

Was she hiding something? Ruby couldn't wait to give Flora a report on her snooping.

The last thing Ruby thought as she finally drifted off to sleep was that she hadn't had an opportunity to peek in her aunt's bedroom.

CHAPTER 12

Still Life

On Halloween morning, true to her word, Ruby arrived at Lacey's house as soon as she returned from her sleepover at Aunt Allie's.

"I'm here!" she announced when Lacey answered the bell. "And I just called Hilary. She's going to come right over."

"My mom's a little mad," Lacey whispered to Ruby as they climbed the stairs to the second floor. "About the costumes. She said she never made anything as complicated as the Eiffel Tower, and now it's going to waste. Except that it isn't really going to go to waste because I talked Alyssa into wearing it in a few years."

"Oh, that's good," said Ruby. "I wish I had someone to give the Leaning Tower of Pizza to. I told Min I could donate it somewhere but she said she hasn't heard of any charities looking for Halloween costumes."

"Well, maybe we can wear them next year," said Lacey brightly. "They'll still fit."

Hilary arrived a few moments later, announced that her parents were cross about the Statue of Liberty costume, and then said, "So. Guess what. I had a great idea. I think we should be three characters from *The Hobbit.*"

"That *is* a great idea," agreed Ruby, "but we'd need a lot of help with those costumes, and believe me, no one is going to help us now. We're on our own. If we're not going to finish the flower costumes, then we need to come up with something simple."

Lacey scrunched up her face. "Something simple," she repeated. "Hmm."

"How about ghosts?" said Hilary.

"Boring," said Lacey and Ruby.

"Beauty queens, then. We could just wear our bathing suits."

"Boring," said Lacey.

"Plus we'd freeze," added Ruby.

"Well, if all the simple ideas are so boring, why don't we just wear the costumes our parents made?" asked Hilary. "They're definitely not boring."

Ruby shrugged. "It's fun to keep changing our minds. Don't you think?"

"But now we've run out of time," said Lacey.

"Hey!" exclaimed Ruby. "I know what we could be and it's really, really unusual and I think we could make the costumes in a couple of hours."

"What?" cried Hilary.

"What?" cried Lacey.

"A still life," said Ruby.

"What's a still life?" asked Hilary and Lacey.

"It's a painting of a bunch of fruit."

Silence fell over Lacey's room.

"I don't see —" began Hilary.

"How are we supposed to —" began Lacey.

"Simple," interrupted Ruby. "Each of us will be a piece of fruit. Like, Hilary could be a banana and Lacey could be a pear and I could be a grape. Or a bunch of grapes. It would be fun. And they would be really cool costumes. I bet nobody else tonight will be dressed as a banana or a pear or a bunch of grapes."

"Well . . . huh," said Lacey after a moment. "I like that idea."

"Me, too," agreed Hilary. "Except I don't want to be the banana. You be the banana, Ruby, and I'll be the bunch of grapes."

Ruby considered this. "Okay."

"All right," said Lacey. "That's settled, then. Now, how are we going to turn ourselves into these pieces of fruit?"

Ruby flopped backward on Lacey's bed. "Actually," she said after a moment, "I think the banana will be the easiest costume. Mostly, I just have to wear yellow. I could wear my yellow leotard and yellow tights — I think I have yellow tights — and Flora's yellow coat. And I'll wear a brown cap on my head. You know how the tops of bananas are always brown. Now, a pear . . . that's going to be a little more difficult." Ruby considered Lacey, squinted her eyes, and said, "How are we going to make you pear shaped?"

"Stuffing?" suggested Hilary.

"Hey! I just got a great idea for the grapes!" exclaimed Lacey. "We'll get a bag of green balloons, blow them up, and stick them all over Hilary." She turned to Hilary. "If you wear brown clothes, then your arms and legs can be the stems."

"Brilliant," said Ruby.

Late on Halloween afternoon, as darkness was beginning to fall and the store owners on Main Street were making their final preparations for trick-or-treaters, Ruby, Lacey, and Hilary bounded into Min's house. "Flora?" shouted Ruby. "Flora!"

"I'm up in my room!" called Flora.

Ruby thundered up the stairs to the second floor, Hilary and Lacey at her heels. The girls were wearing their costumes.

"*Ta-da!*" sang Ruby as she flung herself into Flora's room. She came to a fast stop, and Lacey and Hilary ran into her.

"Hey!" exclaimed Flora. "Hi! Wow . . . look at you guys."

"Do you like our new costumes?" asked Lacey.

"I *love* them," said Flora. "Love them."

"Really?" asked Hilary.

"They're . . . they're *unique*."

Lacey leaned forward and whispered to Hilary, "Is unique a good thing?"

Hilary frowned. "I guess so."

"Gosh. Tell me all about your costumes," said Flora diplomatically, putting down the book she'd been reading.

"We're fruit," said Lacey.

"We're a *still life*," said Ruby sternly. "Banana, pear, grapes," she added, pointing out each in turn.

"Wow. You guys are fabulous." Flora glanced at her watch. "Hey, Lacey, Hilary. Do you two have to check in with your parents before you go to Main Street? If you do, you'd better go home now. It's almost five o'clock."

The girls left and Ruby sat down on the edge of Flora's bed. "What are you going to wear to the dance?" she asked.

"That," Flora replied, pointing across the room to the outfit she'd draped over the back of a chair. "Um, Ruby?"

"Yeah?"

"You know what would be really cool to add to your costumes?"

"What?" Ruby straightened up.

"A sign. I could help you with it. We could make it right now."

"What kind of sign?"

"One that says STILL LIFE. You know, in case some people aren't familiar with, um, art forms. Little kids, for instance, might not know about something as sophisticated as a still life painting. What do you think? Should we make a sign?"

Ruby looked doubtful. "Well . . . okay. I guess so."

"Believe me, it'll be a nice addition to your costumes," said Flora, hurrying to get out her paints.

At six-thirty, the banana, the bunch of grapes, and the pear turned onto Main Street.

Hilary drew in her breath. "Oh!" she exclaimed. "Look at everything." Her gaze traveled up and down the busy street. "I don't understand."

Ruby frowned. "What don't you understand?"

"Well, I *live* on Main Street. I've watched the decorations go up. I know what they look like — the lights, the pumpkins. But tonight the town is . . . I don't know . . ."

"Magical?" suggested Ruby.

"I guess so. Wow."

"That's because it's actually Halloween night, and people are out in their costumes," said Ruby. "It's kind of like on Christmas Eve when everyone comes to town to see Santa arrive. Nothing has changed since the afternoon, but suddenly everything feels different."

"See?" Lacey said to Hilary. "We told you it would be fun to go trick-or-treating on Main Street."

"And I'm only a little sad that Flora and Olivia aren't here," said Ruby.

Lacey and Hilary turned to glare at her.

"I said I'm only a *little* sad! Did you not hear me?"

Hilary took a good look down Main Street before she and Ruby and Lacey stepped inside Dutch Haus. The windows of the stores and businesses were outlined in orange and white lights. Carved pumpkins stood by doorways and everywhere, everywhere were people in costumes. Grown-ups and children and store owners and even dogs. (The dogs, Hilary guessed, were wearing the outfits they'd worn the previous afternoon in Nikki's parade.) During the moments that Hilary and her friends paused outside Dutch Haus, they saw two fairies, a giant parrot, George Washington, a milk shake, and a dog in a cow costume.

Ruby opened the door to Dutch Haus. A woman wearing a red dress, a curly red wig, and a pair of tap shoes appeared before her and held out a basket of candy bars.

"Hey!" exclaimed Ruby. "Little Orphan Annie. That's a good costume, Jeanne." She turned to Lacey and Hilary and said, "We should have been characters from *Annie*. I could have been Annie and you guys could have been orphans."

"*Or*," said Lacey, "one of *us* could have been Annie and *you* could have been an orphan."

"Why should *I* —" said Ruby.

"Girls," interrupted Jeanne, "turn around. Let me see your costumes. Hey, those are great. Crayons! What an original idea."

Ruby whipped out the sign.

"Oh," said Jeanne. "Oh, dear. Well, you are very colorful fruit. Did you all get candy bars? Feel free to take more than one."

Hilary's eyes widened. "Really? We can take two?"

"Yup," said Ruby proudly. "That's another one of the great things about trick-or-treating around here."

"Cool!" said Hilary. "Let's get going. Let's go to all the stores in order. We'll go as far as the square on this side of the street — do they even give out candy at the grocery store?"

"Yup," replied Lacey.

"Excellent. And then we should cross and go down the other side of Main Street and then cross back and end up at the diner. You guys have to see my mom and dad. At first they didn't want to wear costumes, but then they got in the spirit, so now they're dressed as Frankenstein and the Bride of Frankenstein. And guess what," Hilary chattered as the girls left Dutch Haus.

"What?" said Ruby.

"My mom is Frankenstein and my dad is the bride."

Lacey and Ruby giggled.

The Still Life collected lollipops at Verbeyst's, Junior Mints at College Pizza, and handfuls of penny candy at the art supply store. Ruby was variously identified as a canary, a squash, and a pencil. No one had any idea what Hilary was.

"We have to hold the sign up at all times," Ruby announced as the girls pushed open the door to Needle and Thread.

When they did so, it opened soundlessly into a darkened room.

"Min?" said Ruby in a small voice.

The lights flicked on and there were Min and Gigi, dressed as the Wicked Witch of the West and Glinda — and Aunt Allie as Dorothy and Mary Woolsey as a Munchkin.

"Ooh, that was scary," said Hilary, shivering.

"Too scary?" asked Gigi.

"Oh, no. Fun scary."

"Mary!" exclaimed Ruby. "And Aunt Allie! This is a good surprise!"

Aunt Allie held out a bowl of Three Musketeers bars. "Here you go, girls. Your costumes are, um . . ."

Ruby pulled forth the sign.

"A still life. How inventive," said Mary.

The girls continued on the route chosen by Hilary. They saw the Fongs at their studio (Grace was now wearing a ladybug costume) and Dr. Malone in his office. ("Huh," said Hilary. "A dentist handing out candy.") At Time and Again, Sonny Sutphin in a magnificent clown costume gave them licorice whips, and at the library they helped themselves to Mary Janes in a bowl that was sitting in the lap of Mother Goose.

At long last, the girls reached the diner. There were the Bride of Frankenstein and his wife. "Hello there!" said Hilary's father, patting his mountain of hair. "Well, look at the three of you. A rainbow. What a wonderful sur —"

"The sign! The *sign!*" hissed Ruby, and Lacey grabbed for it.

"Not a single person knew who we were unless they read the sign," said Ruby a few minutes later as she and Lacey returned to Needle and Thread.

"I don't care," said Lacey. "This was a great night. Wasn't it a great night? Hilary thought it was better than trick-or-treating in her old town."

Ruby grinned. "Yeah. It really was great. Who cares if people didn't know what we were." She crumpled up the sign. "But you know what? Maybe next year we should be the Eiffel Tower, the Statue of Liberty, and the Leaning Tower of Pizza."

CHAPTER 13

Olivia's First Date

Olivia sat miserably on her bed. Through her open window she could hear trick-or-treaters laughing and shouting as they made their way to Main Street, and she longed to be one of them. She let out a puff of breath and picked at her cuticles.

Olivia had decided that she didn't want to go to the dance at Central.

Why, oh, why had she said yes when Jacob had asked her? The invitation had been exciting, of course, but now that the big night had arrived, Olivia felt certain she had made a mistake. A very big mistake. And gazing at the open door of her wardrobe, inside of which she could see every outfit she had first decided upon and then rejected, she thought that perhaps wearing a costume to the dance wouldn't have been such a bad idea after all. A costume didn't need to be grown-up or cool or perfect. There was nothing right or wrong about a costume. And the idea of wearing a mask was very appealing just now.

"Olivia? Are you ready?" called her mother from the hallway.

Olivia tried to figure out how to tell her mother that she wasn't going to the dance. She hesitated for so long that Mrs. Walter knocked on the door and then opened it just wide enough to poke her head into the room. "Olivia?" she said again.

"No, I'm not ready," Olivia mumbled.

"What's the matter?"

"I don't want to go!"

Mrs. Walter smiled. Then she sat down next to her daughter. "Opening night jitters?"

"What?"

"It's an expression. It means, 'Are you nervous?'"

Olivia nodded. "I don't even know what to wear!"

"I thought you and Flora and Nikki chose something last night."

"We did, but now it looks stupid. And babyish. Which is no surprise since we got it in the little kids' department."

"What's Flora going to wear?" asked Mrs. Walter.

"Jeans and a sort of sweatery thing over a tank top."

"Well, you have jeans and that striped shirt that buttons down the front and a tank top. Come on. You have to get dressed. I told Min we'd pick Flora up in ten minutes."

"I'm not going."

"You've decided to let Jacob and your friends down?"

Olivia sighed. "No."

Her mother gave her a hug. "I'll meet you downstairs."

Ten minutes later, Olivia, dressed in the outfit she and Flora and Nikki had chosen, was sitting in the backseat of the car beside Flora.

Nobody spoke.

Olivia looked out the window at the trick-or-treaters.

"Remember last year?" she said forlornly.

"Oh, for heaven's sake!" exclaimed her mother. "This is a *dance*. You girls are going to have *fun*. And if you get nervous, think of your father and me dressed as Sonny and Cher, handing out candy at the store."

Olivia buried her head in her hands. "I hope nobody from school sees you."

Mrs. Walter let out a sigh of her own. "Does everything we do embarrass you?"

"Life embarrasses me," replied Olivia.

She brightened, though, when they pulled into the school parking lot and found Nikki waiting for them. Nikki was so excited that at the sight of the Walters' car she began to hop up and down.

"There's someone who looks happy about the dance," commented Mrs. Walter. "Now, girls, *please*. Try to have fun."

"You're not a size-two kid in a size-twelve school," muttered Olivia as her mother drove away. But she could hear music drifting through the open door to the gym, and she admitted that she did in fact feel a teensy bit excited. She reminded herself that only seventh- and eighth-graders would be there. And, most important, Jacob had specifically invited her to the dance.

This was her first date.

"Olivia," Flora whispered suddenly. "There he is."

Waiting at the door to the gym was Jacob. He was standing by himself, his collar askew, his hair damp and slightly flattened, as if he had come straight from the shower.

"He's so cute!" exclaimed Nikki in a whisper.

Olivia found herself smiling. And when she approached Jacob, she found that he indeed smelled of soap — and also something sharp, which was not unlike her father's aftershave lotion.

"Hi, Olivia," said Jacob. "Hi, Flora. Hi, Nikki. Olivia, you, um, you look really nice."

"Thanks." Olivia found herself incapable of uttering another word.

"Come on. Let's go inside!" said Nikki.

They entered the gym and Olivia sucked in her breath. "Ohh," she said. "*Look.*"

Olivia had expected to find the room decorated with run-of-the-mill pumpkin cutouts, cobwebs, and orange and black crepe paper. What she found instead was a world of glitter and light. The walls had been hung with sparkly netting. The refreshment tables were strewn with silver sequins and confetti. The teachers were wearing blue-and-silver wizard's caps. And each student who entered the gym was handed a neon glow stick.

Olivia snapped hers smartly and watched it begin to shine a brilliant green. She was about to fasten it around her neck when Jacob said, "Here. Let me do that."

"Thank you," replied Olivia, blushing. Then she leaned over to Flora and whispered, "Hey, look. No one's dancing."

Flora smiled. "I know. I guess we aren't the only shy ones."

Olivia and Jacob, with Flora and Nikki in tow, walked across the gym to watch the band — three boys and two girls dressed entirely in black.

"Who are they?" asked Olivia after a few minutes. "They're good." (She had no idea whether they were good or horrible.)

"They're called Snooze," replied Jacob. "The band members are all in twelfth grade. My brother knows them."

"Snooze," repeated Flora. "You'd think a band would choose a perkier name."

Jacob laughed. He turned to Olivia. "Want to dance?"

Olivia stepped back from Jacob. She looked across the dance floor. She looked at her feet. "Well . . ."

"You know what?" said Jacob. He leaned close to Olivia and whispered, "I don't want to dance, either."

Olivia grinned. "Really?" She let out a rush of breath. "Oh, I'm so glad. I mean . . . well, you know."

Jacob looked as relieved as Olivia felt. "I don't like to dance," he admitted. "At least not when people are watching me. And then I go and invite you to a dance!"

"But it doesn't matter because *I* don't like to dance!"

"Hey!" exclaimed Flora, grabbing Olivia's elbow. "There's Willow. I feel terrible — we should have invited her to come with us. And we didn't even think of it. At least I didn't."

"I didn't, either," said Olivia. She saw Willow standing uncertainly by the refreshment table. "Let's go talk to her."

Olivia, Jacob, Nikki, and Flora walked back across the gym, waving to Willow on the way.

"You came!" said Olivia, just as Flora was saying, "We should have asked you to ride over here with us. I'm sorry we didn't think about it. We're so used to —"

Willow interrupted with a wave of her hand. "Don't worry about it. I couldn't have come with you, anyway. I . . . I had to sneak out. Mom wouldn't give me permission to go to the dance, and I didn't want to miss it. So . . ."

"So you snuck out?" Nikki repeated. "How?"

"Believe me, I've had years of practice. The first thing I did when we moved into the Row Houses was check out escape routes. Well, not escape routes exactly, but you know what I mean."

Olivia had no idea what she meant. She had never once had to escape from her own house.

Jacob looked from Willow to Olivia, then drew Olivia aside. "Does she have a father?" he whispered.

"Yes. Why?"

"Oh. I just wondered. Maybe he's not home or something. Willow said her *mother* wouldn't let her go. But she didn't mention her father."

"Um, Willow?" said Olivia. "What about your dad? Did he say you couldn't go, too?"

"Not in so many words." Willow reached for a cookie. "He just usually goes along with what Mom says. But it's no big deal. Really."

Olivia glanced at Flora and Nikki. She knew that they thought it was a very big deal, and so did she.

"Who's the band?" asked Willow.

"Snooze," replied Jacob, snoring loudly, and everyone laughed.

"I'm going to check them out. I don't want to miss anything." Willow looked at her watch. "Gosh. I still have to figure out how to sneak back in tonight. Sometimes that's harder. Once — hey, who are those girls?" Willow had shifted her attention to a small knot of girls nearby. "Two of them are staring at us," she added, narrowing her eyes.

Nikki whispered, "Melody Becker and Tanya Rhodes. Our mortal enemies. Well, Olivia's mortal enemies."

"Really?" said Willow, looking at Olivia with interest. "You have mortal enemies? What's their problem?"

"Well, at the moment," said Nikki, "they're jealous that Jacob invited Olivia to the dance."

Willow smiled. "Excellent." She reached for another cookie. "Okay. I'll see you guys later."

"Flora!" squeaked Olivia as soon as Willow was out of earshot. "She had to sneak out of the house!"

"That doesn't sound good," said Jacob.

"I sense trouble," added Nikki.

Four pairs of eyes followed Willow across the gym.

"Maybe Min can at least drive her home with us tonight," said Flora.

"Maybe," said Olivia dubiously.

Later, much later, Olivia and Jacob stood side by side at the edge of the dance floor.

"One more song and the dance is over," said Jacob.

"It went so *fast*," said Olivia. "All of a sudden, it went so fast." She glanced around the gym. "I wonder where Willow is."

Olivia and Jacob, soon joined by Flora and Nikki, searched the room but couldn't find her.

"I guess she left already," said Flora uncomfortably. "And, Olivia, I hate to say this, but we have to go, too.

Min's probably waiting outside. Um, I'll meet you in the parking lot. Come with me, Nikki."

Olivia turned to Jacob. "You know what? This is the best dance I've ever been to — and I didn't dance once."

Jacob grinned. "Same here. The best dance ever."

CHAPTER 14

Sewing Day

When the phone rang on the day after Halloween, Flora didn't hear it. She had decided she needed a sewing day and had closed herself into her room. She sat contentedly on the floor in a muddle of patterns, fabrics, buttons, and magazines. The magazines were open to pages featuring outfits Flora liked and thought she could copy.

Flora didn't actually need new clothes. What she needed was the chance to clear her head, and a sewing day was perfect for that. She had realized that her brain was swimming with thoughts of Olivia, Jacob, dances, dates, Min, Mr. Pennington, more dates, Willow, and Aunt Allie's mystery.

When the door to her room burst open and Ruby thrust the phone inside, Flora jumped and knocked over a box of pins that lost themselves in her rug.

"Ruby! Don't you ever knock?" she cried.

"Well, I called, but you didn't answer, and I didn't want Willow to have to wait too long. Why didn't you answer?"

"Can't you guess? I didn't hear you."

Ruby made a face. "Would you like me to put the phone back?"

"No! I just want you to knock before you come in my room."

"Okay, okay. Jeez."

Flora took the phone, and Ruby slammed her door.

"Hello? Willow?" said Flora.

"Yeah, hi. It's me."

"How are you? We were looking for you at the dance last night. We would have given you a ride home."

"Oh," replied Willow. "That's okay."

Flora was desperate to find out how Willow had gotten back in her house but instead asked, "Did you have fun?"

"Yeah, it was great. Everyone here is really nice. I talked to a lot of people and danced with a couple of guys. I don't know their names, but they were nice, too." She laughed. "My mother would have a fit if she knew I had danced with boys and didn't even find out their names."

"So, um," said Flora, "I guess you got home okay last night?"

"Yup. No problem. But sneaking back in always

kind of ruins whatever came before. I feel like Pollyanna when I do it. You know — climbing up the tree to sneak back through her window after the fair? It's a good way to take the magic out of an evening. Hey, Flora?"

"Yeah?"

"I was wondering, would you like to . . . well, I'd invite you over, but it isn't really a very good day around here. Do you want to go into town or something?"

"Today?" Flora looked at her room — at the fabrics, the patterns, the magazines. She knew she should say yes, or at the very least ask Willow to come over to her house, but . . . a sewing day. She didn't get to have them very often, not entire days.

"Well, yeah," said Willow, and Flora could already hear the disappointment in her voice.

"Willow, I'm sorry, I can't."

She was trying to figure out whether to tell Willow about sewing days when Willow said, "That's okay. Really. Some other time. I'll see you in school tomorrow." And she hung up.

Flora sat on the floor, staring at the phone. At last she stood up, opened her door, and handed the phone to Ruby, who, as Flora had suspected, was slouched in the hallway, where she had been eavesdropping. "Here," said Flora, and she retreated into her room.

The conversation had put a slight damper on the

sewing day, but Flora simply added it to the list of things she would mull over as she worked.

She sorted through the magazines again and settled on a dress — a summer dress, but that was okay — that she liked quite a bit. It was sleeveless, with a scoop neck and a complicated back, but what Flora liked best was the combination of fabrics that had been used. The dress looked as though it had been slashed diagonally from the left shoulder to the lower right side, the top part a brilliant peacock blue, the bottom emerald green.

"I bet I could make that," she said aloud. She found a pattern for a sundress that she had made before and pulled out the contents of the package. If she cut the bodice and the skirt pieces in two diagonally, allowing extra fabric for the additional seam . . . yes, that should work. Now — fabric?

Flora began to search through lengths of fabric, thinking of Willow as she did so. She imagined Willow sneaking through a window to get back into her Row House. Then she realized that Willow hadn't said that was how *she* had gotten back in her house; she had said that was how Pollyanna had tried to get back in *her* house. And what was wrong with Willow's mother, anyway? Clearly, something was wrong.

Adults were hard to figure out. Well, *people* were hard to figure out, but somehow Flora found adult shortcomings more troubling than kid shortcomings.

She felt grown-ups should know better. Or at least be more predictable.

Flora's mind wobbled right around to the subject of change again. Which reminded her that Min and Mr. Pennington were going out to dinner that night. Another date. Although Flora personally thought that Sunday was not as romantic a night for a date as Friday or Saturday.

Flora's main concern with the relationship between her grandmother and Rudy Pennington was how things would change if they got married — something her aunt Allie had assured her was not about to happen anytime soon. Still, it *could* happen. And while Flora loved Mr. Pennington, she didn't want to move — into his house or anywhere else. Of course, it would make much more sense for Mr. Pennington to move into Min's house than for her and Ruby and Min all to move into his house, but either way it meant change. And really, thought Flora, did her grandmother and Mr. Pennington *want* such a big change at this time in their lives? Maybe they didn't. But if they didn't, why were they dating? What could come of it? This was a mystery.

Flora wondered what Aunt Allie would think about marriage for Min — a wedding of two rather elderly citizens. And then she wondered about the baby clothes in Aunt Allie's closet. Here was another mystery, and wouldn't you know, it involved another adult. Ruby had said that the closet looked exactly the way it did when she and Flora had discovered it in September. Not a thing was different, at least not so far as Ruby had noticed. And now there was the photo of Allie and the handsome man that Ruby had found in the desk drawer, and the letter with the return address from . . . what had Ruby said? Peru? Mexico? Flora was tempted to ask Ruby about it right that second, but she wasn't ready to abandon her sewing.

Flora sat at her desk and began a list of things she would need for her dress. She was very grateful for the discount Min gave her at Needle and Thread.

She sucked on the end of her pen. "One yard of green fabric," she said aloud. "One and a half yards of blue fabric. Buttons?" She looked at the pattern. No, no buttons.

She set her pen down. She should really, she thought, offer to make some clothes for Olivia. It was awful that Olivia had to shop in the children's department, especially now that she and Jacob were . . . were what? Dating? Were they really dating? Flora felt a pang — an actual pang — in her stomach. You are being uncharitable, she said to herself. *Very* uncharitable. She could hear Min's voice. "And unbecoming," it admonished her.

So why did the thought of Jacob and Olivia bother her? Was it because she wished someone had asked *her* to the dance? No. Well, it would have been nice, of course, but it wasn't something she had wished for, and anyway, she didn't know a single other girl besides

Olivia who *had* received an invitation. Was she upset because Olivia had made a new friend? No. She and Olivia each had a number of friends.

Flora sighed. She suspected she knew what the problem was. When she looked ahead of her, down the hallway of years, past thirteen and fourteen, eighteen, twenty-one, she saw only change. Soon she and the rest of her friends would be invited to dances all the time, and boys would start to call, and Saturdays would be spent not giggling in Needle and Thread nor sitting on the lawn with the other Row House kids, but going to the movie theatre at the mall and to football games and parties. There would be driving lessons and final exams and college applications. And bras — there would be *bras*.

Flora stood and looked out her window at Aiken Avenue. If a genie were to appear from somewhere at that very moment, Flora would ask it (she didn't know if a genie was male or female) to stop time so that she could stay twelve years old having sewing days in her room at Min's house forever.

Or would she? Stopped time meant not being able to solve Aunt Allie's mystery and not getting to know Willow. It meant Nikki wouldn't be able to go to college, which was her dream, and Flora certainly didn't want to take away anyone's dream.

She sat down again, had a sudden inspiration regarding shoulder ties on the sundress, and returned her attention to her project. Before Flora knew it, the morning was over, she had completed the alteration on the pattern, and a feeling of calm had settled neatly into the center of her body.

This was the beauty of a sewing day.

CHAPTER 15

Visiting Day

"Oh, dear. Are you sure we have everything?" Mrs. Sherman surveyed the car, which was parked on the gravel drive, every one of its doors open.

"Positive," replied Nikki. "Look. All of Mae's stuff is on the backseat. Coloring books, crayons, juice box, crackers, her pillow."

"Did you take the books out that she stuck in there? You know she'll get carsick if she tries to read."

"I snuck them out," said Nikki. "Don't worry. And I packed the maps. Really, Mom, I think we're all ready. And remember, this is just a two-hour car ride. It's not like we have to pack for a big, long trip. It's eight-thirty. By ten-thirty we'll be at Leavitt."

"Lord, I hope so. You marked the route on the map, right?"

Nikki nodded. "And Tobias printed out the directions on his computer. *And,*" she rushed on before her mother could say anything else, "I put them on the front seat. I'll be the navigator so you don't have to worry about anything but driving."

Mrs. Sherman drew in a slow breath. "Okay. Where's Mae?"

"I made her go to the bathroom again even though she said she didn't have to. I took Paw-Paw out, too."

"And Min Read is going to drive Flora over this afternoon to walk him?"

"Yup. Okay. Here's Mae. Let's go."

Mae jumped down the porch steps, two books falling from inside her jacket as she did so.

"Books," said Nikki harshly. "Put them back, Mae."

"Oh, ding-dong," said Mae, but she retreated into the house.

"Lock the door behind you!" Nikki called as her sister returned empty-handed.

Nikki, Mae, and their mother slid into the car, three doors slammed, and the Shermans' road trip was under way.

"Let's sing 'Ninety-nine Bottles of Pop on the Wall,'" called Mae from the back as Mrs. Sherman steered down the driveway.

"No!" yelped Nikki and her mother. Then Nikki added, "We have to concentrate. Look, Mom got you a new coloring book. Why don't you make some pictures for Tobias? He can put them up in his dorm room."

"What's a dorm room?"

"It's where kids sleep when they go to college," said Nikki knowledgeably.

"Are they bedrooms?"

"Yes."

"Then why don't they just call them bedrooms?"

"Mae, really, I have to help Mom here. Open your coloring book."

Two hours later, with Mae fast asleep and Nikki bent over one of the maps, Mrs. Sherman called out, "There's a sign for Leavitt College!"

"See? Tobias's directions were perfect!" exclaimed Nikki. "Oh, this is so exciting. Just two miles. We're almost there."

"Now, what did Tobias say to do when we reach . . . Beacon? Is that the name of the town?"

"Yeah." Nikki consulted a note from Tobias. "Okay, um, we're supposed to turn left at the first traffic light, park anywhere on High Street, and then look for Coffee Joe's. It'll be next to a bookstore. That's where we're going to meet him. At Coffee Joe's, I mean, not the bookstore."

"Goodness, my heart's pounding," said Mrs. Sherman. "I can't believe we've come this far."

"Without any mistakes," said Nikki.

"You'd better wake up Mae," added her mother, peering into the rearview mirror. "She's going to need Crabby Time to recover from her nap."

As Mae grumbled in the backseat, squinting into the sunlight, Nikki took a careful look at Beacon. The edges of town were unimpressive — strip malls and gas stations and fast-food restaurants. Then her mother made a right-hand turn, drove to the traffic light, and turned left, and suddenly Nikki found herself looking down a stretch of road that could have been Main Street.

"Ooh," said Mae, perking up. "A toy store."

"This is just like Camden Falls!" exclaimed Nikki.

"It's lovely," said her mother.

"Look, there's a parking space and it's right in front of Lighthouse Books — and there's Coffee Joe's, just like Tobias said!"

A smile spread across Mrs. Sherman's face. "We did it," she whispered.

"Yay, Mommy," said Mae.

Nikki eased out of the car, stretching her legs, and found herself face-to-face with her brother. "Tobias!" she exclaimed.

"Hey there, little sister." Tobias wrapped Nikki in a bear hug.

"Tobias! Tobias! Look what I made for you!" Mae scrambled out of the backseat with a fistful of pages from her coloring book. "You can hang them in your boardroom!"

Tobias looked confused, and Nikki whispered to him, "She means your dorm room."

"Oh. Thanks!" he said. He leaned down to peer through the window into the front seat. "Hi, Mom," he said. "You made it."

She smiled at him. "Thanks to Nikki."

"Let's go to Coffee Joe's before we head back to campus," said Tobias.

"Great. I could use a cup of coffee," said Mrs. Sherman, heaving a sigh as she extricated herself from the car.

Mae let out a sigh of her own. "Me, too," she said. And added, "Man, I'm beat."

"You slept almost the whole way!" cried Nikki.

"And since when do you drink coffee?" added Tobias. "Or say, 'Man, I'm beat'?"

"Since I got to college." Mae marched through the door of Coffee Joe's, stepped up to the counter, and said, "One coffee, please."

Joe leaned across the counter and peered down at Mae. Then he glanced at Nikki, Tobias, and Mrs. Sherman, who had hurried in after her.

"Sorry," said Mrs. Sherman. "That will be two coffees, one milk, and . . . what do you want, Nikki?"

"Iced tea, please."

"Hey! Is that milk for *me*?" squawked Mae.

"Yes, and settle down, please," said her mother.

Nikki sat on a stool and took a good look around Coffee Joe's. Plastered on the walls were fliers advertising poetry readings, concerts, recitals, and plays. "Tobias, you could do something different every single night in Beacon," she said. "Look — there's going to be a performance of *Our Town*. We read that in school. It was the best play ever. And a group called Split the Bill is going to play right here at Coffee Joe's. Who's Split the Bill?"

"Two women who sing and play the guitar," Tobias replied. "They're really good."

"This is *so* cool." Nikki sipped her iced tea. "I love college."

"And you haven't even seen Leavitt yet," said Tobias.

When they finally did — when they had finished their drinks, made sure their car was locked, and walked along the road that led up the hill toward campus — Nikki drew in her breath. She knew, even before she had let the breath out, that she would never, ever forget this view of Leavitt College. The old brick buildings seemed to rise up out of green lawns like a fleet of ships appearing on the horizon.

"Here's the main entrance," said Tobias as they walked through a set of ornate iron gates. "These gates were built in eighteen seventy-four, the year the first part of the campus was finished. That big building just ahead is the Jeffers Science Center. Over there is Neilson Hall. That's where all the English classes are held. That new building is the student center. Across the lawn is the main library, and right behind it is the music library. The performing arts —"

"Wait!" interrupted Nikki. "That huge building is the *library*? And there's another library, too?"

"There are three other libraries," said Tobias proudly.

"How can there be so many *books*?" wondered Mae, who had seen only the library at Camden Falls Elementary and the tiny public library on Main Street.

"Do you want to look inside?" asked Tobias.

"Are we allowed?" whispered Nikki.

"Of course."

After Nikki and Mae and Mrs. Sherman had gawked at the shelves and shelves and floors and floors of books, Mae, once again growing giddy with excitement, said, "Now can we see your boardroom, Tobias, please?"

So Tobias walked his family past the performing arts center and the student center to a group of six buildings, each four stories high, that formed a U around an expanse of lawn. He strode purposefully to a building on the left, led the way to a door on the second floor, swung the door open, and said, "Home, sweet home."

Nikki looked in at the messiest suite of rooms she had ever seen. Clothing was tossed everywhere, including, in one case, on a lamp shade. ("Fire hazard," she announced, whipping the shirt off the shade and folding it neatly over the back of a chair.) She and her mother and Mae had to pick their way from one room to another, sidestepping books, empty pizza boxes, computer cords, paper plates, and crumpled napkins.

"Don't you boys eat at a table?" asked Mrs. Sherman.

But Nikki decided the rooms were wonderful, the happy result of life lived far from the eyes of parents.

Tobias looked at his watch. "If we go to the student center now, we can meet my roommates and their families," he said. "We thought it would be nice if we all ate lunch together."

Nikki saw concern cross her mother's face and knew Tobias saw it, too. She took her mother's hand. "It'll be fun," she assured her. "And if it's not, we'll leave."

But it was fun. Nikki liked Bruce and David, her brother's roommates. She liked their parents, too. So what if the moms were wearing tailored pantsuits while her own mother wore a skirt that Nikki suddenly realized was just a bit too short — and makeup that had been lathered on a bit too thickly? When talk turned to ski trips and to Bruce's parents' summer-house on Martha's Vineyard, Mrs. Sherman merely refilled her coffee cup. And everyone was indulgent of Mae, who insisted on being called Goldie and went around the table telling fortunes.

When lunch was over, Nikki asked to continue the tour of campus and was enthralled when Tobias took her and Mae and their mother to a green-house, a real theatre, playing fields, and even a small art museum.

"This," said Nikki as her family walked back to town later that afternoon, "has been one of the best days ever. I'm going to come to Leavitt after high school, just like you, Tobias. I'll do anything to get here. I'll make straight A's, I'll get a scholarship, whatever it takes."

"Listen," said Tobias, "if I could get in, then you'll get in for sure."

"That," said Nikki, "is my new goal. I'm not going to lose sight of it."

And she never did.

CHAPTER 16

House Arrest

Vincent Barnes tucked his copy of *When Zachary Beaver Came to Town* under his arm and left the Teachers' Room.

"See you tomorrow," called Mr. Krauss, one of the math teachers.

"Have a good evening," Mr. Barnes replied. He whistled as he walked through the halls of Central. He was beginning to feel a part of the school and a part of Camden Falls, his new community.

This afternoon it was time for another meeting of the seventh-grade book club, and Mr. Barnes was looking forward to it. The students in the club had held one meeting to determine how the book club should run, a second meeting at which they had chosen their first book (*Bud, Not Buddy*, by Christopher Paul Curtis), and a third meeting at which they had talked about *Bud, Not Buddy* and chosen *Zachary Beaver*, by Kimberly Willis Holt, as their next selection.

"Hi, Mr. Barnes!"

"Hey, Mr. Barnes, how's Shortbread?"

"Mr. Barnes, I couldn't find the book in the library until yesterday, so I had to read the whole thing in one night!"

Mr. Barnes looked at the group of kids crowded outside the door to his classroom. They were full of smiles and energy and ideas, his most motivated students.

He grinned at them. "Nikki, you read that whole book in one night? No wonder you have bags under your eyes."

"What? I don't have bags under my eyes! Do I, Olivia? Well, anyway, it was worth it. That was the best book ever."

"That's what you said about *Bud, Not Buddy*," said Mr. Barnes, holding the door open.

"Mr. Barnes?"

Vincent Barnes turned around at the sound of the shy voice behind him. "Hi, Flora." He glanced at the unfamiliar girl standing next to her.

"Mr. Barnes, this is Willow Hamilton," said Flora. "Is it all right if she comes to the meeting? She just moved here and she wants to join the book club. Olivia and Nikki and I have been telling her about it."

"It's fine with me." Mr. Barnes smiled at Willow. "Did you have a chance to read the book?"

Willow nodded. "I'd read it once before, but I reread it over the weekend, anyway."

"Excellent."

Mr. Barnes ushered Flora and Willow into the classroom and then sat at his desk. He paged through *Zachary Beaver* while the rest of the students trickled into the room. Snatches of conversation reached him.

"She gave us a pop quiz! It was completely unfair."

"Karen said that *Janey* said that Oliver wants to go out with Pam, but she doesn't want to go out with him."

"Olivia! Sit over here!" That was Jacob. Mr. Barnes knew it without looking up.

But he did raise his eyes when he heard a voice say, "I'm not even supposed to be here. I'm under," the voice was lowered, "house arrest."

The voice belonged to Willow, and when Mr. Barnes glanced at her, she looked down at her desk, cheeks reddening.

"Everything all right?" Mr. Barnes asked her.

She nodded.

Mr. Barnes hesitated. "Okay," he said, and Willow gave Flora a sideways look, then sagged in her seat.

The room was full now. Every desk was taken, and several students were sitting on the floor. "Are we all here?" asked Mr. Barnes. "Anybody missing?"

When no one answered, he said, "Today we're going to talk about *When Zachary Beaver Came to Town*. As you know, my policy is to stay in the background. Does someone want to lead off, or would you like me to ask a question to get things started?"

A forest of hands shot into the air, and Mr. Barnes smiled. "Amy?"

"Okay. Well, how about if I begin by summarizing the book? We started last month's meeting with a summary," said Amy Adams. When no one objected, Amy went on. "All right. Um, *Zachary Beaver* is about what happens when the fattest boy in the world — that's Zachary, only it turns out he isn't really the fattest boy — comes to Antler, this small town in Texas, one summer. He affects a lot of people's lives, especially the lives of Toby and Cal. Toby's the narrator," Amy added.

"What I liked," said Jacob, "are the people in Antler. Some of them have small parts in the book, but they leave big impressions. Like Miss Myrtie Mae."

"At first," said a boy sitting against the back wall, "I couldn't tell what Toby's intentions with Zachary were. Like, I thought he was going to be mean to him. And actually, he *was* kind of mean to him, but then things changed."

Mr. Barnes held up his hand. "Excuse me, I have to interrupt. Why do you think that happened?"

There was silence. Then Flora said, "I think Toby began to identify with Zachary. They were both outcasts. And also, they had both been abandoned. Toby had been abandoned by his mother, and Zachary had been abandoned by Paulie Rankin." Flora paused. "And in a way, by his own mother when she died."

Mr. Barnes had learned enough about his students to know that Flora had lost her mother — and her father — less than two years earlier.

"You know what's interesting?" Willow spoke up.

"Excuse me. I'm sorry to interrupt again," said Mr. Barnes. "I seem to be breaking my own rule today. But for those of you who don't know her, this is Willow Hamilton. She's new here at Central. Okay, Willow. Go ahead."

"Well, I was just thinking that we don't even get to meet two of the most important characters in the book."

Mr. Barnes grinned. "Good point."

But several of the students said, "What? I don't get it."

"Think about it. What does Willow mean?" asked Mr. Barnes. "The reader doesn't meet two of the most important characters in the book. Who's important but never actually appears?"

"Ooh, ooh! I know!" cried Olivia. "Wayne. We never get to meet Cal's brother. We just hear his letters."

"Oh, then Toby's mother must be the other one," said Nikki. "She calls Toby once, but we don't really meet her."

"That's pretty interesting, isn't it?" said Mr. Barnes.

"Characters can have an impact on a story even when they're almost," Willow paused, "almost invisible."

"Yes," agreed Mr. Barnes, regarding Willow thoughtfully. He was mentally taking notes on Willow now, and the first two were *Under house arrest* and *Feels invisible?* When he realized that her eyes continually strayed to the door of the classroom, he added, *Is she waiting for someone? Is she afraid of someone?*

Eventually, Mr. Barnes's own eyes drifted, not to the door of the classroom but to his watch. "I think we're going to have to wrap things up," he said. "You have about fifteen minutes in which to choose your next book and then we'd better go."

It was Willow who suggested the book that was ultimately agreed upon: *Homecoming*, by Cynthia Voigt. "It's about a mother who abandons her kids," said Willow, and Mr. Barnes added another note to his list.

"All right," said Mr. Barnes. "Great meeting. Have a good evening."

As the students left the room, some in a hurry, some hanging back to laugh and talk, Mr. Barnes gathered up the papers on his desk. He kept one eye on Willow, though, and watched her as she was surrounded by Flora, Olivia, and Nikki, and the girls made their way to the door. Willow was still a foot or two away from it when an arm snaked into the room and yanked her into the hallway.

Nikki, Flora, and Olivia jumped, and Flora emitted a gasp. But Willow said only, "Mom," in a very low voice, and Mr. Barnes heard the quiet edge of resignation in the word.

"What are you doing here?" Mrs. Hamilton asked Willow sharply. "You're under house arrest. Have you forgotten?"

Mr. Barnes stepped into the hallway. "Excuse me," he said. He extended his hand. "I'm Mr. Barnes. I teach English here. May I help you?"

The bluster leaked out of Mrs. Hamilton. She didn't accept Mr. Barnes's outstretched hand, but she let go of Willow. "No," she said. "No, thank you. I just . . . I just need my daughter. Willow, come on, please."

Willow followed her mother down the hall. She didn't look over her shoulder. Mr. Barnes thought he could feel anger in Willow's footsteps. He turned his attention to Olivia, Nikki, and Flora, and was about to ask Flora a question when she waved self-consciously to him and disappeared down the hall with Nikki and Olivia, keeping a safe distance behind the Hamiltons.

Mr. Barnes knew the seventh-grade guidance counselor at Central only slightly. He returned to his desk, opened his computer, and considered composing an e-mail to her. But before he had typed a single word, he closed the computer and walked down the hall to her office. He wondered whether anyone had had a chance to look closely at Willow Hamilton's transfer records. He felt sure he would find a notation about her family situation.

CHAPTER 17

Rules

Flora, Olivia, and Willow walked down Main Street one Friday afternoon. They scuffed their feet through the last of the autumn leaves, which were falling, tired and dull and sad, from several towering oak trees.

"The leaves look like they just ran out of energy," remarked Willow as one drifted in front of her and landed at Olivia's feet. "They couldn't hang on anymore."

"I guess in a way that's true," said Flora. She stooped to pick up the leaf and twirled it on its stem. "Can you believe winter's almost here? It feels like it was just summer. But in a couple of weeks we'll be on Thanksgiving break."

"Yum," said Olivia. "I can't wait. We're going to my grandparents' for Thanksgiving this year."

"To . . ." Willow paused. "To Gigi's?"

"No, to my other grandparents'. But Gigi and Poppy will be there, too. What are you guys going to do?"

Flora grinned. "Mr. Willet invited Min, Ruby, Mr. Pennington, Aunt Allie, and me to come to Three Oaks for Thanksgiving. He said they give this enormous, fancy dinner there. Turkey and gravy and stuffing and pumpkin pie. Everything!"

"Cool," said Olivia. "What about you, Willow?"

Willow shrugged. "We haven't made any plans yet."

"Oh." Olivia stopped in front of Sincerely Yours. "Well, I'll see you guys later." She disappeared through the door, ready to start her afternoon of work.

Willow looked longingly through the window.

"Want to go in for a few minutes?" Flora asked her.

Willow shook her head. "No. I was just thinking that Olivia's really lucky. I mean, to have a job and" (she waved at Mrs. Walter, who had come out from behind the candy counter to give Olivia a hug) "well, she's lucky, that's all."

They continued down the street, and when they reached Needle and Thread, Flora opened the door and stuck her head in. "Hi, Min!" she called. "I'm going home now."

Min, who was ringing up a customer, signaled to Flora to come inside. "Hi, girls," she said a few moments later as the customer left with her purchases. "Flora, what do you want to do about dinner tonight?"

"Well, I know what Ruby will want to do."

"Pizza?"

"Pizza."

"I think we've had enough pizza lately. Is chicken okay with you? I could pick one up on the way home. Just turn the oven on at five o'clock, and I'll take care of everything else."

Flora hugged Min across the counter, then hurried out of the store.

"Is your grandmother always like that?" asked Willow.

"Like what?"

"So . . ." Willow scrunched up her face, thinking. "So calm," she said at last.

Flora shrugged. "I guess. Well, actually, she's gotten, um, calmer, as Ruby and I have gotten older. We're allowed to be home by ourselves now, and sometimes we cook a little." The girls left Main Street and a few minutes later turned onto Aiken Avenue. "Willow? Can I ask you something?" said Flora, and without waiting for an answer, she continued, "Whatever happened with house arrest?"

Willow made a face. "It's over. I mean, Mom forgot about it."

"She forgot about it? But it sounded like such a big deal."

"Listen, don't try to understand my mother. No one understands her. Not even my father."

Flora frowned. "Well, what were you under house arrest for?"

"An, um, infraction."

"Of?"

"Just my mom's rules."

"But what did you *do*?" Flora paused, suddenly realizing that she sounded a bit like ghoulish Ruby, eager for all the details of someone's misfortune. "If it isn't too personal," she added lamely.

Willow muttered something about doors, and Flora decided not to press the point. When the girls were standing in front of the Hamiltons' house, Flora looked at her watch and said, "Hey, Willow, you're home later than usual. Is that going to be all right with your mother?"

"My mom's not here. She won't be home for about an hour. She took Cole to the mall to get his hair cut." Willow sounded quite pleased about this.

"Are you sure she isn't home?" asked Flora.

"Positive. Why?"

"Could I come in? This was the Willets' house for so long and, I don't know, I just wondered what it looked like now. I could tell Mr. Willet about it the next time I'm at Three Oaks."

"Well . . . okay," replied Willow. She led the way along the path to the front door. As she searched through her purse for her house key, she said, "Take your shoes off, okay?"

"Take my shoes off?" Flora repeated. When Willow didn't answer, Flora removed her sneakers by stepping on the heel of each one with the toes of the other foot. She waited in her sock feet while Willow unlocked the door and stooped to take off her own shoes, which she carried into the hall. Then she leaned back outside to arrange Flora's sneakers so that only the heels were touching, the toes pointing in opposite directions as the shoes formed a severe line.

Flora was about to ask her what she was doing when again an image of nosy Ruby nudged its way into her head. She kept her mouth shut.

Flora stepped into Willow's house. "Gosh, it's dark —" she started to say, then stopped herself. "But it looks really nice with all the shades down. It's, um, cozy."

"No, it isn't," replied Willow. "It's claustrophobic." She shrugged her shoulders and spread her hands as if to say, "But what can I do about it?"

Flora poked her head into the Hamiltons' living room. "This is just like our house," she told Willow. "I mean, you have the same floor plan. The houses on either side of you are opposite. They're mirror images. Olivia explained that to Ruby and me one day."

"Has Olivia lived in the Row Houses all her life?" asked Willow.

"Yup. She was born here. So was her mother. So was my mother. So was Min, for that matter."

"Wow. That is so cool."

Flora was busily looking around, taking in everything so she could give Mr. Willet a detailed report when she saw him. The very first thing she noted was that the living room was as neat as a pin. Not a single thing was out of place. Throw pillows were arranged symmetrically on the couch. A lamp was positioned in the exact center of each end table. There was not a speck of dust in sight. Flora thought of her own living room. When she had run by it on her way out the door that morning, she had noted vaguely that she and Ruby had left an unfinished game of Monopoly on the floor. King Comma wasn't in the room, but Flora could see where he had been sleeping because he had left a ring of black fur on a green couch cushion. Two half-gnawed bones belonging to Daisy Dear lay before the fireplace. And Min's knitting spilled out of its bag and onto an armchair.

"Boy," said Flora, gazing around Willow's living room, "this is like a museum or something. What I mean," she added hastily, "is that our living room is kind of messy. And Mr. Willet left magazines and books everywhere."

"Want to see my room?" Willow asked.

"Sure," Flora replied, craning her neck to look into the Hamiltons' dining room, which, as far as she could tell, was every bit as tidy and spotless as the living room. If she hadn't known that Willow and Cole lived here, she would have assumed this was a house without children.

Willow led the way upstairs, and it was while Flora was following her down the hallway that the doors attracted her attention. In all the tidiness, she now realized that every single door in the house — closet doors, bathroom doors — stood open, each at an exact ninety-degree angle to the wall. It was the one thing that made the house look not so tidy. What better way to hide a mess than to close it into a closet? As they passed the linen closet (which immediately made Flora think about the closet in Aunt Allie's house), she reached out and shut the door.

Willow opened it again, carefully adjusting it to its previous position. Flora wouldn't have been surprised if she'd pulled a protractor out of her pocket to get the angle just right.

A strange feeling was coming over Flora, and she stopped trying to memorize rooms for Mr. Willet, focusing instead on everything about the house that seemed somehow wrong to her. The uneasy feeling inched down her body on whispery spider's feet.

She peeked into closets (how could she not peek, when all their doors stood wide open?) and noticed that every pair of shoes was lined up not side by side but heel to heel, as Willow had positioned Flora's sneakers on the front stoop. Willow's bedroom, Flora then noticed, had all the personality of a hotel room.

Cole's, too. Flora would never have guessed that either room belonged to a kid. She was trying to convince herself that this was just because the Hamiltons had so recently moved in, when Willow led the way back downstairs and into the kitchen, and Flora saw the table. It was already set (for supper, she supposed), but every single plate and glass, every fork and spoon, was turned facedown.

Flora could contain herself no longer. "Um, Willow? How come . . ." She thought about how to phrase her question without sounding rude and started over. "I noticed that in your closets," she said, "your shoes are lined up . . . differently than I line mine up. And" (she glanced at the table) "when we set —"

Willow interrupted her. "These are just my mother's rules, okay?" she said quietly. "Nobody understands the rules any better than they understand my mother."

Flora felt heat creeping up her face. "I'm sorry," she said. She couldn't think of anything to add to that and miserably repeated, "I'm sorry." But why, she wondered, had Willow allowed her to come inside and look around if everything was so strange? Flora tried to imagine never letting anyone inside her own house. Impossible. And then another thought occurred to her. Perhaps Willow *wanted* someone to see all the strange things. Perhaps she was asking for help.

The front door opened then and Willow let out a yelp. "That must be Mom! She's home early."

"Willow!" called Mrs. Hamilton from the hallway.

"Come on," said Willow grimly. She took Flora by the wrist and led her out of the kitchen and into the front hall. "Hi, Mom," she said.

Mrs. Hamilton, shoeless, was hanging her coat in the closet. Cole, also shoeless, was disappearing upstairs.

"Willow!" exclaimed her mother. "I didn't know you were going to have a friend over."

"I was just leaving," said Flora, making a dash for the door.

Mrs. Hamilton stepped in front of her. "Did you tap the vase?" she asked Flora. She turned to Willow. "Did she?"

Flora glanced nervously around the hall and her eyes fell on a large and probably very expensive porcelain vase standing guard by the front door. "No!" exclaimed Flora. "I didn't touch anything."

Mrs. Hamilton now leveled her gaze on Flora. "You *didn't* tap it," she said flatly.

"No . . ." said Flora. She felt behind her back for the doorknob.

"So Willow didn't tell you the rule."

Flora raised her eyebrows at Willow.

"No, I didn't tell her the rule." Willow sounded tired.

"But . . . but the rule is that anyone who comes in the house — *any*one — *has* to tap the vase five times!" Mrs. Hamilton sounded panicked. "Did Willow tap the vase?" she asked Flora. "Did she? Were you the only one who didn't tap it? Tell me Willow tapped it."

By this time, Willow had crossed the hall and was standing next to Flora. Before Flora could answer the question, Willow said, "I tapped it, Mom. Don't worry."

Flora, who was certain that Willow had done no such thing, added, "I'll tap it now."

"Now is too late!" cried Mrs. Hamilton.

Flora hesitated no longer. She twisted the knob, pulled the door open, and escaped onto the stoop. As she leaned over to pick up her shoes, she whispered to Willow, "You have to tell someone. If you don't, I'm going to tell Min."

Willow slumped against the door. "I'll talk to my father tonight," she said.

CHAPTER 18

Dinner for Two

Flora had seen very little of Willow's father since the Hamiltons moved in. She didn't know whether Willow would talk to him, and if she did talk to him, Flora had no idea whether he'd listen. So she vowed to tell Min everything that had happened, and to do it the moment Min walked through the door after work.

Those were the thoughts tumbling through Flora's head as she pelted across the Malones' yard and up the steps to her own front door. She thrust herself inside, realizing as she did so that Ruby must already be at home, since the door wasn't locked.

And if that was the case, Flora shouldn't be smelling what she smelled as she slammed the door shut behind her.

Something was cooking on the stove, and Ruby wasn't allowed to use the stove when she was at home alone.

"Ruby?" Flora called.

"In the kitchen!"

Flora made her way through the living room and came to a halt as she entered the dining room. "What on earth?" she said softly.

Ruby emerged triumphantly from the kitchen. She was wearing a chef's hat and holding a wooden spoon in one hand. "What do you think?" she asked.

"I —"

"Are you speechless?"

"I —" said Flora again. "Yes, I'm speechless."

"Cool. I made you speechless."

"But, Ruby, what are you *doing*?" Flora looked around at the dining room. Ruby had set the table with Min's best china, crystal, and silver. The fanciest (and whitest) of Min's lace cloths rested gracefully on the table, and by each plate lay a lace napkin. In the center of the table was a vase full of straggly autumn flowers that Flora had a suspicion Ruby might have cut from Mr. Pennington's garden. The vase was flanked by candlesticks, each holding a brand-new white candle.

The table was set for two people.

"Ruby, what is this?" asked Flora. "What's going on?"

"It's for Min and Mr. Pennington. I planned a surprise for them. See, what I did was, I phoned Mr. Pennington this afternoon and asked him if he could come over at six o'clock for dinner, and he said yes. But I didn't tell him it was dinner for two, so he's going to be really surprised. And Min doesn't know anything about it at all. She's going to be even more surprised."

"I'll say," murmured Flora. She sniffed the air. "Ruby, I smell stuff cooking, and you know you're not supposed to use the stove when I'm not here."

"Well, where *were* you?" said Ruby accusingly. "You were supposed to be home by now."

"I know, but I —"

"But you were sup*posed* to be. I can't help it if you're late. You need to be more dependable, Flora."

Flora sighed. "The house didn't burn down, so that's good. What are you serving tonight?"

Ruby disappeared into the kitchen and returned holding a piece of paper. "Here's the menu," she said. "Read it out loud, okay?"

"Okay. Let's see. 'Friday, November Thirteenth.'"

"That's the only bad part," interrupted Ruby. "That today is Friday the thirteenth. It sort of casts a spell, or whatever you call it, over dinner. I hope it doesn't mean that something terrible is going to happen."

"Oh, I'm sure it doesn't. And by the way, your menu looks very fancy."

"I chose a different font for every single line of the menu," announced Ruby. "Okay. Keep reading."

Flora cleared her throat. "'Special dinner for two for Mindy Read and Rudy Pennington.' Ruby?"

"What?"

"How come you're doing this?"

"Doing what?"

"*This.* Fixing a romantic dinner for Min and Mr. Pennington."

"I just thought it would be nice."

"Ruby . . ."

"Okay. And I wanted to hurry things along."

"Hurry them along toward what exactly?" asked Flora.

Ruby looked at the kitchen floor. "I don't know. A wedding?"

"Ruby!"

"Well, everything is going too slowly. It's taking forever, and I want to be the flower girl. But pretty soon I'll be too old to be a flower girl."

"If you're too old, you can be a junior bridesmaid."

Ruby stamped her foot. "You don't understand! I want to be a flower girl! I've never been one. Opportunities are starting to pass me by. I'm too old to be the littlest orphan in *Annie*. I'm too old to be Gretl and probably even Marta in *The Sound of Music*. And if the community theatre doesn't put on *Mary Poppins* in the next year, I'll be too old to be Jane Banks. It's all slipping past me — and I'm only ten. Min *has* to get married soon. I don't want to miss my shot at flower girl."

"Are you planning this dinner for Min and Mr. Pennington or for yourself?" asked Flora.

"I — it's — never mind. Just finish reading the menu."

Flora looked back at the piece of paper. "All right. 'First course — Campbell's Tomato Soup. Second course — olives. Main course — fish sticks and SpaghettiOs.'" She paused. "Fish sticks. Is that what I smell cooking?"

Ruby nodded. "I guess I started them a little early."

"No kidding," said Flora. "Okay. 'Dessert — Pop-Tarts.' Wow. Ruby, this is really something. I'm . . . stunned."

Ruby grinned. "Good."

"I have just one suggestion. Don't you think Min and Mr. Pennington might want something green with their meal?"

"The olives are green."

"I mean lettuce or a vegetable. Most grown-ups like vegetables with their dinner."

"Well . . ."

"And also, maybe we could come up with something different for dessert. Mr. Pennington might not like Pop-Tarts."

"Might not like Pop-Tarts! Who doesn't like Pop-Tarts?"

"Well, again, grown-ups."

"But I don't have time to redo the menu!" Ruby said explosively. "It took me an hour to do that one."

"We could just make additions — surprise additions — to the meal," said Flora diplomatically. "We'll give Min and Mr. Pennington some things that aren't on the menu. I'll help you make a salad and you can serve it with the olive course, okay? And maybe we could serve ice cream with the Pop-Tarts."

Ruby narrowed her eyes at Flora. "How come you're being so nice? I know you don't want Min and Mr. Pennington to get married. Not yet, anyway."

Flora sighed. "You're right. But I do want Mr. Pennington to have a nice meal. So let's embellish things, okay?"

Ruby sat down on the dining room floor with a plop. "This is not how I wanted things to go!"

Flora looked at her watch. "Stand up," she commanded. "You don't have a whole lot of time to finish getting ready. Let's take the fish sticks out of the oven and put them in the fridge. You can stick them in the microwave just before you're ready to serve them." She sniffed thoughtfully. "You didn't heat up the soup already, too, did you?"

"Yes," said Ruby.

"All right. We'll put the pot in the fridge with the fish sticks. Now, what do you want me to wear? You're going to wear your chef's outfit, aren't you?"

"Yes. And I want you to wear your velvet dress. The one from last Christmas."

"Fine. Let me go change. I'll be back downstairs in a minute."

Ruby thought of all the hopeful, optimistic songs she knew, and finally admonished herself that she was never fully dressed without a smile. Another song, one from *Bye Bye Birdie*, came to her, too, and she said out loud, "So put on a happy face."

Then she returned to the kitchen to straighten out her dinner.

At precisely six o'clock, the doorbell rang.

"That's Mr. Pennington!" cried Ruby. "Are you ready, Flora? Oh, you look nice."

"Thank you. And you look very chef-y."

Ruby flung open the door and greeted Mr. Pennington. Moments later, Min arrived.

"Surprise!" exclaimed Ruby. "Look!" She took Min by one hand and Mr. Pennington by the other and led them into the dining room. The drapes were drawn, the candles were lit, and the lights had been dimmed.

"My stars and garters," said Min.

"I planned it all — just for you!" announced Ruby. She thrust the menus at them.

"'Special dinner for two,'" read Mr. Pennington. "Well, isn't this something?"

"I had a little help from Flora," said Ruby. "But mostly I did this myself. Okay. Now, Min, you sit here, and Mr. Pennington, you sit here around the corner from Min. Isn't that how they do it in fancy restaurants? The two people don't sit across from each other, they sit next to each other, or on the corner like this. Ready for your first course?"

"Ruby," said Flora in a loud whisper, "let them get settled first. Mr. Pennington is still wearing his coat."

Ruby slowed down a bit, but by six-thirty the dinner was over.

Mr. Pennington leaned back in his chair and patted his stomach. "My, my. That was excellent."

Ruby noted that he had not, in fact, eaten his Pop-Tart. But his ice cream dish was empty. Flora was kind enough not to point that out to her, though.

"Well, well, well," said Min.

Hmm. Six-thirty. Ruby had not expected the romantic dinner to be over quite so quickly. She stood on a chair to make an announcement. "And now," she said, "for the entertainment portion of the evening." She eyed her sister. "Flora, could —"

"No! I am not doing any kind of performance. You go perform and I'll clean up the kitchen."

"Really?"

"Yes," said Flora, sounding vastly relieved.

Ruby led Min and Mr. Pennington into the living room, settled them side by side on the couch, sang four numbers from *Annie*, and performed a tap number as well.

She had no idea that in just an hour the thoroughly pleasant evening would come to an end with a frightening jolt.

CHAPTER 19

Out of Control

That evening, while Ruby cooked and served and performed for Min and Mr. Pennington, Flora's thoughts were mired in her afternoon at Willow's house. She had intended to greet Min that evening and immediately share the horrifying news with her, but she didn't want to spoil Ruby's plans, and she didn't think a few hours would make much difference, anyway. After all, poor Willow had lived with her mother for twelve years. So Flora tried to forget about Mrs. Hamilton and enjoy the hours with her grandmother and her sister and Mr. Pennington.

"Why don't we play a board game?" suggested Mr. Pennington after Ruby's performance was over.

"That's a lovely idea," agreed Min. "Girls?"

"Let's play Sorry," said Flora.

"Charades," said Ruby.

"No! Too much acting!" cried Flora, looking stricken. "Besides, charades isn't a board game."

"Min, you choose something," said Ruby.

Min chose Life, and they set up the game on the kitchen table.

An hour later, Mr. Pennington was winning — and gloating — when Flora cocked her head and said, "Do you hear sirens?"

Everyone held very still, and a moment later Ruby said, "I hear them!"

"It must be a fire," said Mr. Pennington.

"Remember last summer," said Ruby, "when the diner burned down? That was an exciting night."

Min frowned at her.

"Well, it *was* exciting. Come on. You have to admit it."

"The sirens are getting louder," remarked Mr. Pennington, and he stood and opened the back door. "I think they're closer."

"They don't sound like fire engines," said Min.

"I think they're on our street!" cried Ruby. She dashed through the house to the front door and flung it open.

Flora was right behind her. And she was moving so fast that when Ruby came to a stop, Flora stepped on her heels.

"Ow!" Ruby screeched.

Flora ignored her. "Look," she said. She pointed toward Dodds Lane as two green-and-white Camden Falls police cars careened around the corner and turned onto Aiken Avenue. To her amazement, they drew up (in a great hurry) in front of the Row Houses, and in a flash, doors opened and three officers leaped out and walked briskly across the lawn.

"They're going to the Hamiltons'!" said Ruby.

Flora felt her stomach turn over. She whirled around to call Min but found that her grandmother and Mr. Pennington were standing behind her, leaning through the doorway.

"Uh-oh," said Flora, beginning to tremble. "Min, I was going to tell you something. It's really awful —"

"Honey, I think whatever it is will have to wait."

Min was staring at the Hamiltons' house and Flora followed her gaze. She saw Willow and Cole huddled on their stoop, Bessie beside them, Willow's arm protectively across her brother's shoulders. With her free hand, Willow signaled to the officers.

"Oh, my lord," said Min softly.

"What's happening?" whispered Ruby, now sounding frightened.

"Do you think we should offer to help?" asked Mr. Pennington.

Min hesitated. "They might want their privacy. We don't know what's going on."

It was at that moment that Flora heard screams from inside the Hamiltons' house, and Willow suddenly tugged her brother down the steps and partway across the lawn. They were followed by a trembling Bessie.

"An ambulance!" said Ruby then, her breath coming quickly. Flora put her hand on her sister's back and realized Ruby was shivering.

An ambulance was indeed on the way. It came from the direction of Main Street and turned onto Aiken Avenue so fast that Flora truly thought it was going to topple over. It didn't, of course, and it pulled up behind the squad cars.

"There's Mr. Hamilton," said Mr. Pennington.

The front door had opened and Mr. Hamilton had burst through it, calling, "Willow! Cole!"

"We're right here, Dad," Willow replied, and when her father caught sight of them, he put his hand over his heart, then ran to them and hugged them tightly in a great trembling embrace.

"I think we'd better go offer to help after all," said Min. "Rudy, will you come with me? Girls, you stay right here. *Right here.* I mean it."

"Yes," Flora and Ruby said instantly.

Flora didn't take her eyes off of her grandmother and Mr. Pennington. She watched them hurry across the lawn and along the sidewalk to the Hamiltons' house. Min hesitated just briefly before taking Mr. Pennington's hand and approaching Willow and Cole and their father. One of the police officers joined them then. Flora couldn't hear what was said, but moments later, Willow and Cole hugged their father again and, with Bessie in tow, followed Min and Mr. Pennington back to Flora's house.

"*Pssst!* Flora!"

Olivia, clad in a flannel nightgown, appeared next to Flora, and Flora jumped and nearly stumbled down the steps.

"Sorry," said Olivia, who didn't sound sorry at all.

Flora looked up and down the street and realized that Aiken Avenue had come to life. Couples stood on porches, blinds were raised, and a small knot of people was gathering on the sidewalk. Robby Edwards, also dressed in his pajamas, jumped up and down in his yard while his father spoke to the Fongs. Olivia's parents were peeking out of their front door, simultaneously peering down the street and trying to keep Henry and Jack inside.

"What is it? What happened?" Olivia asked breathlessly.

Flora shook her head. "I don't know. We heard screams coming from the Hamiltons', and now Min is bringing Willow and Cole back here."

"I can't wait to find out —" Ruby began to say.

But Flora hushed her. "You can't ask a lot of questions. It isn't polite. Just let them say whatever they want to say. They look scared to death."

Min and Mr. Pennington guided Willow and Cole to the stoop, where Flora, Ruby, and Olivia waited. Flora noted that Willow kept her head down. Cole was crying.

"Inside, everybody," said Min matter-of-factly. "Olivia, I think you'd better come back in the morning."

"I'll call you," Olivia whispered to Flora, and she ran next door.

"Willow, Cole," said Min, "do you know Mr. Pennington? He lives two doors down."

Before Willow or Cole could answer, Bessie and Daisy caught sight of each other and burst into ear-splitting barking. King Comma ran up the stairs with such speed that all Flora caught sight of was the tip of his tail as it disappeared over the top step.

"Bessie!" cried Willow. "No!"

Ruby grabbed Daisy's collar. "Daisy, where are your manners? Bessie is your guest."

Cole sat down in the middle of the hall and cried silently, his face buried in his hands.

"Flora, can you manage the dogs?" asked Min as she took Cole by the hand and guided him to his feet. "I think Cole and I will see about making hot chocolate."

"Perhaps I should go home," said Mr. Pennington quietly. "Min, would you like me to take Daisy for the night?"

After a hasty discussion, Mr. Pennington left without Daisy, promising to call first thing in the morning. Then Min led Cole into the kitchen, Ruby closed Daisy into Min's bedroom, and Flora and Willow settled Bessie on the couch with one of Daisy's bones.

"I — I didn't say anything to Min yet," Flora told Willow.

Willow brushed her hand across her eyes. "Well, everyone is going to know now."

"Know what now?" Min had returned to the living room, followed by Cole. She was carrying a tray with five mugs of hot chocolate.

Cole looked at his sister. "You can't tell," he said.

"Dad is talking to the police, so it's all right," Willow replied.

"You don't have to tell us anything, though," said Min. "Not if you don't want to. But you do need to tell me if you're injured. Is either one of you hurt? We heard screaming, so you have to tell me if you're hurt."

"That was my mom," said Willow. "She was screaming. But no one is hurt. I promise."

"The problem is Mom's rules," Cole spoke up.

"No, it's more than that. The rules are a symptom of an illness," said Willow.

"She's not sick," replied Cole, looking confused.

"Yes, she is. Her mind is sick. Your mind can get sick just like your body can. And Mom's mind is sick." Willow turned to Min. "She's been sick for a really long time. Since before I was born. But it didn't used to be so bad." She paused. "It's hard to explain."

"Why don't you begin at the beginning?" said Min gently.

"It's even hard to know where the beginning is." Willow glanced at Cole.

"Maybe we'll talk about this later," said Min. "Ruby, you take Cole to the guest room and show him where everything is. Maybe you can choose a book to read."

Cole carefully placed his half-full mug on the tray and followed Ruby upstairs.

Willow drew Bessie into her lap and said, "I don't know exactly what's wrong with Mom. I mean, she's mentally ill, but I don't have a name for her illness. I remember that when I was really little, she was a nice mom who played with me and read to me and made me laugh. But then Cole came along and little by little Mom changed. The rules started a few years ago." When Min raised her eyebrows, Willow said, "She has all these rules that don't make any sense. She says we have to leave the closet doors open and they have to be exactly perpendicular to the walls. And we have to line up our shoes a certain way, and there's this vase by the front door that we're all supposed to tap whenever we come in the house. At first everything was sort of okay. As long as we followed the rules, she was, you know, calm or whatever. But lately there have been more and more rules. She makes up new ones almost every day. We can't remember them all, and then she gets so mad at us. It's out of control. I mean, Mom is out of control."

"Does she see a doctor?" asked Min.

"You mean a shrink?" replied Willow. "Yeah. She used to, anyway. She went two or three times a week. But she hasn't found a new doctor since we moved here."

"Do you think the move made things worse?"

Willow nodded, and suddenly tears were dripping down her cheeks and dropping into her lap. Min held out her hand, but Willow shook her head. "Flora, can we go upstairs now?"

"Sure." Flora led Willow to the second floor. "That's the guest room," she said, pointing down the hall. She could hear low voices and had a feeling Ruby was reading to Cole.

"Okay. Flora? Do you want to know what happened tonight?"

"If you want to tell me."

"I do."

Willow and Flora sat on Flora's bed and Willow said, "All Cole did was shut his closet door. The door rule is new and we have trouble remembering it. Anyway, after dinner, Cole went to his room to play on his computer and a few minutes later, Mom checked on him and saw that the door was closed and she just started screaming and yelling. And then she was throwing things and punching things and kicking the walls. She couldn't stop. Cole was crying and Bessie was growling and Dad tried to talk to her, but he couldn't quiet her down. Finally, he called nine-one-one." Willow gazed blankly out Flora's dark window.

"It's been bad before, but nothing like this has ever happened."

"Maybe now your mom will get some help. Whatever it is she needs," said Flora. "Maybe a new doctor?"

"Maybe. You know, the funny thing is that as awful as tonight was, I feel like things might change. I think they're going to get better."

"What's going to happen now?"

Willow shrugged. "Mom will go to a hospital. I guess she'll stay there awhile. And . . . it'll just be Dad and Cole and me at home. That will be a relief."

Flora had a lot more questions for Willow and was trying to form a tactful one about Mr. Hamilton, when there was a knock on the door and Cole said, "Willow? Will you come to bed now?"

"We can talk some more in the morning if you want," said Flora.

Willow threw her a grateful but exhausted look.

When Flora turned out her light that night, she lay in her bed for a long time, listening to the silence.

CHAPTER 20

A Quiet Day

Olivia had trouble falling asleep that night. She had never witnessed anything like what she had witnessed at the Hamiltons' earlier in the evening. She remembered the day when Min had called to say that Flora and Ruby had been in an accident and that their parents had died. And she remembered various sad times, and the previous year's uncertainty when her father had lost his job and her parents had thought that perhaps they would move away from Camden Falls. But an out-of-control mother? The police screeching onto Aiken Avenue in the dark of night? Screams blaring from inside the Hamiltons' house of secrets?

Olivia wanted to believe that nothing like that could ever happen to her family. But when it happened to people living just three doors away, well . . .

Olivia shivered. She drew the covers up to her chin and then all the way over her head. She wished she had a cat or a dog so she could invite it to join her in her bed cave. She knew that sometimes King Comma crawled into bed with Ruby, curled up just behind her knees, and purred warmly there for hours. How comforting that must be. Olivia stretched out her hand and touched the wall. On the other side of that wall was Ruby's bedroom. And somewhere down the hallway in Min's house were Willow and Cole Hamilton. Were they asleep yet? Olivia didn't think *she* would be able to sleep if she were Willow. She thought she would lie awake in bed the whole night remembering the sound of her mother screaming and screaming, the sight of the police officers rushing across the lawn and of her father looking frantically for her and her brother, afraid they had been hurt.

Olivia shivered again. Then she told herself to clear her head of bad thoughts. Eventually, she fell asleep remembering Daisy Dear in the dog parade, an image that made her smile.

The next morning, Olivia awoke to a day that was remarkably clear and sunny, but that also made a very loud announcement that winter had arrived. Olivia's first clue was when her feet hit the bare floor and she found it icy cold. She raised her window shade and saw frost in the yard. "It must be freezing out today," she said to Sandy, her guinea pig, who was peering at her from within a cardboard house that Olivia had recently fashioned for his cage. She rubbed her skinny arms. *"Brrr."*

Her thoughts turned to Willow and Cole and the events of the previous evening, and she wondered how early she could call Flora.

She settled on nine o'clock.

Flora answered the phone. "Min's taking the day off from the store," she reported. "Willow is still asleep, and Ruby and Cole and I are having breakfast. Want to come over?"

"Where's Mrs. Hamilton?" Olivia wanted to know. "Did Mr. Hamilton call you guys yet?"

"Well, as I said, Ruby and *Cole* and I are having breakfast," Flora replied pointedly.

"*Oh*, I get it. You can't talk. Well, take the phone out of the kitchen."

"Olivia!"

"Okay, okay. I'll come over."

"You know what? Why don't you bring Jack and Henry with you? They can play with Cole today."

"To take his mind off things?"

"Yup."

"All right. They're still eating breakfast, but we'll be there in a little while."

Jack and Henry happily accompanied Olivia to Min's house that morning.

"Gosh," said Ruby a little later, looking at Cole, Jack, and Henry as they turned the living room into a battleground and took aim at one another from behind the couch and armchairs. "There aren't usually so many boys in this house. Isn't there something else boys can do?" she asked Olivia. "I'm not sure Min is going to —"

Ruby was interrupted by the stern presence of Min, who marched into the room and announced that there would be no fighting and no weapons of any sort, imaginary or otherwise, in the house. Then she produced a stack of board games. To Ruby's surprise (but not Olivia's), the boys pounced on Operation and decided to play a championship series. Olivia left the room to the sound of shrieks and an annoying buzzing, and Ruby hustled out of the Row House, on her way to a rehearsal of the Children's Chorus.

"Come upstairs," said Flora.

Olivia and Willow followed Flora upstairs to her room, Flora closing the door in order to drown out the buzzing and shouting from below.

"So," said Olivia, dropping to the floor and leaning against Flora's bed, "are you okay, Willow? I thought about you for a long time last night. I was really worried."

Willow, who was settling herself in Flora's desk chair, let out a sigh. "Yeah. I guess. My dad called a little while ago. He's going to pick Cole and me up this afternoon. He spent the night at the hospital."

"Your mom is in the hospital?"

Willow nodded. "Not the one that's nearby, though. This one's — well, I don't know exactly where it is, but it's not too far away, I guess. It's the nearest one that has a good, what do you call it? Psychiatric wing."

"Oh," said Olivia, reddening as she realized that she had been about to suggest the term "mental ward." "And your mom's going to stay there?"

"Yup. I don't know for how long, but probably for a few weeks. Maybe even a few months."

"Has your mom ever stayed in a hospital before?" Olivia asked. "I mean, not because she was sick but because of her . . . problems?"

Willow frowned. "I remember her going away once when I was little, for a short time. Ever since, she's just seen doctors and tried medications and stuff. And for a while, those things seemed to work."

"Willow?" said Flora. "Can I ask you something? And if it's too personal, just say so. I won't be offended."

"Okay," said Willow.

"Well, it's about your dad. How come he doesn't do anything about your mom's rules —"

"What rules?" interrupted Olivia.

Willow told Olivia what she had told Flora and Min, then said, "It's not like Dad was ignoring them. It's just that I think he didn't know *what* to do. And anyway, the rules didn't get really bad until recently. Then we moved, which made them worse, and Dad was starting his new job and he wanted it to go well, so he was spending a lot of time at the office and not much time at home. But now I think things are going to be different. Can I tell you something?"

"Sure," said Olivia and Flora.

"I know this sounds funny, but sometimes the littlest things are the scariest ones."

"What do you mean?" asked Olivia.

"I mean that last night was terrifying, of course. It was so over the top. The police, Mom screaming and breaking things . . . but if you ask me, it's even scarier to come downstairs and find my mother standing in the living room just staring."

"You mean, thinking?" asked Flora.

Willow shook her head. "I mean literally staring. Standing and staring at a pillow or a chair leg or a coaster. Like this." Willow got to her feet and stood in the center of Flora's room, staring in a concentrated and slightly hostile fashion at a sneaker.

"That's creepy," said Olivia in a small voice a few seconds later. She let out an involuntary shudder.

"I know," replied Willow. "Then there was the day she decided Cole and I needed protection."

"From what?" asked Flora.

Willow shrugged. "Not a clue. I can't figure out what goes on in Mom's mind. But she said we needed protection, and she told us to sit on her bed, and then she surrounded us with things she chose very carefully from the room — her engagement ring, the hair dryer, a postcard that was on my dad's bureau, a sock. None of these items meant anything to me, but I guess they did to Mom. She treated them as if they were talismans, placing them around us almost reverently. It was all very quiet and peaceful. There was hardly a sound in the room, and Mom seemed so serene. After Cole and I had sat inside the circle of charms, or whatever they were, for about five minutes, Mom put them all away, told us we were protected, and let us go back to our homework.

"Anyway, it's things like the staring and the ritual that, when I think about them, scare me even more than last night."

"But now," said Olivia, trying to sound hopeful, "your mom is in the hospital."

Willow nodded. "Yes. And I have a good feeling about it. I really do. Maybe I shouldn't. I mean, maybe I shouldn't get my hopes up. But I think that what happened last night is going to change things. We'll all get a break from Mom, and Dad will be in charge for a while. I know he'll figure out how to handle his new job and take care of Cole and me, too. He really is a very good dad," said Willow. "*Really.* But it's hard for anyone to take control when Mom's around. Now he'll have the chance. I kind of hope that Mom won't come home for a while. Like for a few months. It would be sad if she was away for Thanksgiving and Christmas, but Cole and Dad and I need time to ourselves. I feel like we've just been coping with Mom instead of really trying to, you know, make a life here."

"Hey, I have an idea!" said Olivia suddenly. "We should all go into town. The three of us and Nikki. We haven't had a chance to do that yet. It would be so much fun."

"I'd like that," Willow replied. "Maybe not today, since I want to be here when my dad comes back, but how about tomorrow? I'm pretty sure he'll let me go."

"That would be great!" exclaimed Flora. "There's so much we haven't shown you yet."

"You haven't met horrible Mrs. Grindle," said Olivia.

"Do I want to?" asked Willow, smiling.

"And you haven't hung out at Needle and Thread," said Flora. "Sometimes Min and Gigi let us work there — and they pay us."

"I like to operate the computer," said Olivia. Then she added, "Willow? Don't you miss your old town?"

Willow shook her head. "I never felt like I belonged there, or anywhere we've lived. I spent all my time trying not to upset Mom. It was exhausting. But now — here's my chance to start over and to be able to concentrate on belonging somewhere."

"Camden Falls is a pretty nice 'somewhere,'" said Olivia.

At three-thirty that afternoon, the doorbell rang and Cole Hamilton practically fell down the stairs in his effort to answer it. "It's Dad!" he cried. "I saw him from Ruby's window!" He flung the door open. "Dad! Dad!"

Mr. Hamilton pulled Cole into a fierce hug and then reached for Willow, who had followed Cole down the stairs. Olivia, Ruby, and Flora stood at the top of the steps, glancing at one another. "Min," whispered Flora, as Min emerged from her sewing room. "He's back."

Min and Willow's father talked for a long time in the kitchen before the Hamiltons returned to their home.

"When will Mrs. Hamilton come back?" Ruby wanted to know, sounding apprehensive rather than ghoulish.

Min looked at the three faces — Ruby's, Flora's, Olivia's — that had turned to her. "Not for quite a long time," she replied.

"After the holidays?" asked Olivia.

"Probably."

Olivia and Flora exchanged a glance. "That's good," said Olivia.

"Why?" demanded Ruby.

"It just is," said Flora. "It's a good thing."

CHAPTER 21

A Saturday Adventure

One morning in November, Flora awoke early and lay in bed doing some counting. Suddenly, she sat up and exclaimed, "Oh, no! Only thirty-six more days until Christmas!"

"What?!" shrieked Ruby from across the hall. Only the mention of Christmas could yank Ruby from a sound sleep so early in the morning.

"Girls?" called Min from down the hall.

Flora was on her feet now, studying her wall calendar. "Thanksgiving is next week, and, yup, I was right. Only thirty-six days until Christmas. That means even fewer shopping days. And I haven't done *any* shopping. Or made anything — well, hardly anything. I was going to make a whole bunch of my presents." Flora drew in her breath. Then she let it out. "Thirty-six days," she repeated in surprise. "How did that happen?"

Min appeared in Flora's doorway, yawning and tying the sash of her faded pink bathrobe around her

179

generous waistline. "Christmas snuck up on you?" she asked.

"I'll say," replied Flora.

"Well, you've had a pretty busy fall."

"That's true." Flora flopped onto her bed. "New school, Mr. Willet moved, the dog parade," she said, counting on her fingers. "The Halloween dance, new neighbors . . ."

"And not your average neighbors at that," interjected Min.

"No." Flora reached for Min's sash and wound it around her hand. "Willow visited her mother yesterday," she said. "Cole didn't go. He didn't want to. But Willow and her father did."

"And how was the visit?"

Flora shrugged. "Willow didn't say much about it. Just that her mother wasn't agitated. She said her mom is on new medication and she's getting therapy — I don't know what kind — but that she isn't ready to come home. Willow seemed really relieved about that part."

"My understanding," said Min, "from talking to Mr. Hamilton, is that Mrs. Hamilton won't be home until February at the earliest."

Flora nodded. With Mr. Hamilton in charge, the second Row House from the left was a happier place. The shades were raised, Willow and Cole could come and go as they pleased, and their friends were welcome. Closet doors were left closed — or open, there was no longer a rule about them — shoes were strewn haphazardly about the house, tables were set with plates and utensils right side up, and a nice messiness had overtaken Willow's and Cole's bedrooms. The vase in the front hall had temporarily been moved to the garage, since Cole said it scared him. Willow was a regular member of the book club and was becoming friends with Claudette Tisch and Mary Louise Detwiler. And she and Flora and Olivia had made several trips to Main Street, where one afternoon Willow had helped out at a Needle and Thread sewing class for six- and seven-year-olds.

Ruby appeared sleepily in Flora's doorway. "What are you guys talking about?" she asked, and yawned widely. "I thought Flora was upset about Christmas shopping or something."

"We got a bit off the subject," said Min.

"Oh." Ruby bit down on the wad of bubble gum she was already chewing. "Well, I got a great idea. We should have a Saturday adventure this weekend. We could start our shopping at the same time."

Flora raised her eyebrows in interest. "Speak," she said.

"I was just thinking," Ruby began, "that it's been a while since we had one of our adventures."

"Not since September," Flora agreed.

The Saturday adventures had begun the previous June, when an anonymous someone had created a secret summer book club to entertain Flora, Ruby, Nikki, and Olivia — secret because the girls didn't learn, until midway through August, the identity of the mystery person. Every few weeks, all summer long, someone had sent four copies of a book to the girls and arranged for a Saturday adventure in connection with the book. When the summer ended and the mystery person was revealed, the girls decided to continue having Saturday adventures anyway, just the four of them, the members of the book club. The last adventure had taken place a few weeks after school had started.

"Well." Ruby puffed herself up with importance, then ruined the image completely by blowing a large bubble, sucking it back into her mouth, and cracking her gum loudly. "Here's what I was thinking: On Saturday we could go to the mall — *Bingham* Mall," she added, looking daringly at Min. "By ourselves. And stay there the whole day. By ourselves. We could get lots of shopping done, and have lunch, and maybe go to a movie. By ourselves."

"And how would you get all the way out to the mall?" asked Min.

"Well, not by ourselves," admitted Ruby. "Even I know that's too far. Someone would have to take us there and pick us up. But could we do it? Please? Please, please, please?"

"It *would* be fun," said Flora, excitement mounting.

"You've never been to the mall alone," said Min. "It's ten miles away. I don't know."

"What if we took a cell phone with us?" suggested Flora. "So we could call if anything went wrong."

"And we would promise to stay together the whole time. We would never split up or go off by ourselves," added Ruby.

"I'll have to talk to Nikki's mother and Olivia's parents," said Min.

Flora nodded. "Thank you," she said solemnly, and nudged Ruby, who was about to start begging again. "We'll go along with whatever you decide." She pinched Ruby to keep her quiet.

By Saturday, everything had been arranged. The adults had agreed that the four members of the secret book club could spend the day at the mall as long as they followed certain rules. Mr. Walter had turned his cell phone over to Olivia (who knew exactly how much it would cost to replace the phone if she lost it). Min was to drive the girls to the mall in the morning and Mrs. Walter would pick them up in the afternoon.

"This is going to be the best day of my life!" announced Ruby, who had said that many times in her life.

At precisely eleven o'clock on the Saturday before Thanksgiving, Min Read pulled up to the main entrance of Bingham Mall and dropped off four excited girls, one of them self-consciously responsible for her father's cell phone.

"We'll call you if anything goes wrong!" Flora assured Min.

"But nothing will go wrong," said Ruby gaily.

"We'll check in with you once an hour," added Nikki.

"And we'll be waiting right here at four o'clock," said Olivia.

Min sat uncertainly behind the wheel of her car. "Be careful with your money," she said. "Hold tight to your purses. If you feel you're in danger, go to the nearest store clerk or find someone from mall security." She hesitated a few seconds longer, then pulled into the parking lot and headed for the exit.

"Now I'm a little scared," said Ruby.

"Don't be," replied Olivia. "She's just doing what grown-ups have to do. My mom said all those same things to me before I left this morning."

"Yeah," said Nikki. She turned around to face the glass doors, which were adorned with green garlands and a large red bow, and waved her hand in a swooping arc. "Look! The world of the mall awaits. Let us enter the magic kingdom of consumerism."

Flora held one of the doors open and her friends walked through it. They entered a wide hallway lined with rather boring-looking businesses (a vision center, a dentist's office, and a place for mailing packages), a row of strollers for rent, and a door marked SECURITY.

"Now we know where Security is," said Ruby nervously.

Flora took her sister's hand. "This is going to be fun, Ruby," she said. "We're here on our *own*. We've always wanted to come here on our own. And anyway, look over there."

Flora pointed down the hallway, and Ruby, Olivia, and Nikki let out a simultaneous gasp. Then Ruby began to run. The others ran after her. When Ruby reached the end of the hall, she found herself at the center of the mall. And the mall had been decorated for Christmas.

"It's —" Ruby turned around and around, looking above her (the mall was three stories high) and in all directions. "It's — well, it really is like a magic kingdom."

Flora leaned over and whispered to Olivia, "An incredibly tacky magic kingdom."

The mall appeared to have been dipped in silver glitter and then to have fallen into a bag of candy. Shimmering snowflakes were suspended from the ceiling, drifts of sparkly cotton snow covered the inner courtyard, angels (also shimmering) hovered above, and everywhere Flora looked she saw giant gumdrops, candy canes, chocolates, lollipops, peppermint drops, licorice whips, and gingerbread men.

Ruby was still trying to put her thoughts into words. "It's kind of like Main Street if Mr. Freedly went crazy when he was putting up the decorations."

"Oh, let's be realistic," said Nikki finally. "It's insanely overdone. But who cares? It's also really fun. Look, there's Santa's house in the middle, in all that snow."

"Where?" said Ruby. "I don't see it."

"Behind those two big snowmen," said Nikki, and then she let out a scream. "*Aughh!* One of them just moved! I didn't know they were alive."

"I wish I weren't too old to visit Santa," said Olivia.

"You aren't," Flora told her. "No one is. We could visit Santa."

But the girls looked at the line of children waiting to enter the sparkly gingerbread cabin that apparently housed Santa Claus, and saw only two kids who appeared to be their age.

"The kids who are leaving the house have candy canes and puzzles," Ruby noted wistfully.

"Well, *we* have shopping to do," said Flora. She pulled a list out of her purse, then snapped the purse shut quickly and looked all around her, Min's words coming back to her. Finally, she consulted the list. "Gosh," she said. "Even if I get around to making a lot of my presents, I still need to buy things for Mr. and Mrs. Willet, Mr. Pennington, Willow, Cole, maybe Mary Louise and Claudette, and a bunch of dogs. I think I'll make catnip toys for King Comma and Mary Woolsey's cats, though."

She looked up from her list to see that Olivia, who was consulting a list of her own, was blushing furiously. "What's the matter?" she asked.

"Well — um, it's — well — I don't —" stammered Olivia.

Ruby leaned over and peeked at Olivia's list. "Ha! Olivia's wondering if she should buy Jacob a present!"

"I've never bought a present for a boy before," Olivia whispered, as if she might turn around and find a group of boys standing sternly behind her, judging her gift-choosing abilities.

"You have *brothers!*" exclaimed Ruby.

"That's not the same."

Nikki, trying hard not to laugh, finally said, "You don't have to make a decision today. You can just look around, okay? Come on, you guys. Let's get going. We have the whole day ahead of us. And I'm already getting hungry. So let's shop a little first and then go to the food court."

"Oh! Oh!" exclaimed Ruby as they set off. "Look what's playing at the multiplex. That dog movie! I really want to see that!"

The Saturday adventure had begun. Flora and her friends followed every one of the rules their parents had laid out. They used Mr. Walter's cell phone, which Olivia guarded like a treasure, to call Min and Gigi at the store once an hour. They stuck together. And they fiercely protected their money and their purses.

Flora had a successful morning of shopping, and the girls enjoyed a lunch of pizza and frozen yogurt in the food court. They continued their shopping after lunch and then checked the times the movie was playing.

"We could see the next show," said Ruby. "But you know what I'd rather do after all? Go get a soda or something and just sit and talk."

And that's what they did. They found a quiet table by a glittering white Christmas tree, sat down, and looked through their purchases.

"This is nice," said Ruby. "We don't get to do so much of this anymore."

"Of what?" asked Flora.

"*This*. Being together, just the four of us. I don't see you guys at school this year, and we're starting to have other friends and do different things. So this is just . . . really nice." She turned to Nikki. "Do you ever hear from your dad?"

Nikki shook her head. "He sent us some money, but he hasn't called or anything. Hey, did I tell you I visited Tobias at school?"

"You went to his college?" said Ruby. "Cool."

"Ruby," said Flora, "tell Nikki and Olivia about the Thanksgiving concert."

Ruby did, and the afternoon spun away.

As daylight faded, Mr. Barnes, armed with a shopping list of his own, entered the mall and walked toward his first destination, the music store. He passed through the food court, and this is what he saw: Four girls sitting around a table, their heads bent, talking earnestly, Flora Northrop's arm around a younger girl. Mr.

Barnes considered stopping to greet his students, but as he neared their table, he heard Flora say, "I hope we can always have days like this," and so he left them to their adventure — they did seem to be on an adventure of some sort — their laughter ringing out behind him.

CHAPTER 22

Winter

This is Camden Falls, Massachusetts, on the evening of the Saturday before Thanksgiving. The day is gloomy, but most people don't care. The dark skies and frosty air feel wintry, and that seems appropriate since the holidays are close at hand. The tourists who explored town this afternoon found Main Street windows aglow in the fading light, decorated with a curious jumble of paper turkeys and cornucopias, droopy witches and graying ghosts. Main Street is a bit behind Bingham Mall when it comes to Christmas decorations; Mr. Freedly's work won't begin until next Saturday. The last vestiges of Halloween can still be seen, and in the window of Camden Falls Art Supply, an old back-to-school banner is still clinging to the glass by the tape on one corner. But the air is humming with the excitement the holidays bring, and everyone is feeling festive.

There's Sonny Sutphin calling good-bye to his co-workers at Time and Again and wheeling himself through the doorway and down the sidewalk. He has fastened a wreath to the back of his wheelchair and looks very jaunty as he crosses Main Street, whistling softly to himself. As he passes Needle and Thread, he waves to Min and Gigi, who are getting ready to close the store. They wave back to him, calling, "Good night, Sonny!" This year for the first time in ages, Sonny will be going to a real Thanksgiving dinner — he's been invited to join Mr. Freedly and his family — instead of dining by himself in his kitchen with a football game on the TV for company.

Walk a bit farther down Main Street, cross Dodds Lane, and pause before the Marquis Diner. A sign in the window reads OPEN FOR THANKSGIVING. Hilary and Spencer are disappointed by this — they long for the kind of Thanksgivings they used to have — but they understand that things have changed since their parents opened the diner. Besides, they've been promised a turkey dinner of their own at home after the diner has closed.

Go back to Dodds Lane, turn right, then right again onto Aiken. Here are the Row Houses, a friendly fortress in the deepening darkness. In the nearest one, the Morrises are starting to get ready for the enormous family dinner they'll be hosting, and the children have been put to work making decorations for the table.

Lacey is in charge of place cards and she colors away busily until Travis peers over her shoulder and says, "Hey! You spelled your own name wrong!"

Next door, the Hamiltons are preparing to go away for the weekend. They've decided not to spend the holiday in their new home. (The Malones will be away, too, and so will the Fongs and the Edwardses.)

The fourth house from the left is buzzing with energy. Flora and Ruby, home from their adventure in the mall, are waiting for Min to return (at this very moment, Min is locking the door of Needle and Thread and calling good-bye to Gigi), and they are in a great state of excitement about the upcoming holiday.

"I can't, can't, can't, wait, wait, wait for the Thanksgiving concert!" cries Ruby as she bounces down the stairs. "It is going to be so excellent! I'm so happy that Lacey and I *both* have solos."

"I'm going to wear my new outfit," replies Flora with satisfaction.

"The one you made?"

"I made half of it — the vest. Min made the pants. Velvet pants. I don't know how she did it. Velvet is *so* hard to work with."

Ruby regards King Comma and Daisy Dear, who are curled up at opposite ends of the couch in the living room. "Remember when they were scared of each other?" she asks.

"Now they're buddies," says Flora.

"It's a Thanksgiving miracle," says Ruby.

Next door, Olivia is in her room with her door partially closed. From downstairs she can hear pots clanking as her mother, who has come home early from Sincerely Yours, begins cooking dinner. Olivia opens her desk drawer and withdraws from it the card she has read over and over in the past two weeks. It's from Jacob, a birthday card, and the message is simple: *Happy Birthday, Olivia. Love from Jacob.* The word "love" is the one Olivia keeps studying and also is the reason she believes she will keep the card forever. She sighs and returns the card to the drawer, taking care to slide it under a stack of papers. She's eleven now, eleven at last. She's not sure what difference this makes, since her body is as skinny and straight as ever, but at least she *is* eleven.

Next door to Olivia, Mr. Pennington is seated contentedly in an armchair. He has decided to reread some of the classics, and his copy of *Bleak House* is open in his lap. He scratches Jacques's ears absentmindedly as he reads.

Leave downtown Camden Falls behind now. Several miles out on one of the county roads lies the home of Nikki Sherman and her family. It is a happy place on this evening. Mrs. Sherman has come home from Three Oaks early (she'll have to work half a day on Thanksgiving, but only half a day), and Tobias has called to talk about Thanksgiving plans. Mae is chattering to him on the phone. "Remember when we visited you and I ordered coffee?" she cries. Nikki feels contentment wash over her. Only four days until Tobias will come home and the long holiday weekend will start.

Travel several miles in a different direction from Camden Falls and you'll find Three Oaks resting placidly at the edge of a small woods, the trees now bare. Mr. Willet is feeding Sweetie in his kitchen before he goes downstairs to join Mary Lou for supper. "Thanksgiving soon," Mr. Willet tells the cat. "And we'll have five guests for dinner." Mr. Willet, whose apartment looks as settled as if he had moved in years ago instead of weeks ago, thinks happily of the holiday. The tables in the Three Oaks dining room, he has been told, will be covered with white linen cloths and decorated with vases of chrysanthemums, and Mr. Willet plans to add a chocolate turkey to each setting at his table. "All the fun of Thanksgiving and none of the cooking," he tells Sweetie.

Back in Camden Falls there is a house with just one person living in it and just one light on. The person has been hard at work all day, but now is about to spend a relaxing evening. The computer has finally been shut down and the desk cleared when the phone rings. The person sighs. It's too late in the day for more work. But the call is not about work. It's from someone this person has spoken to only once before. And what the caller says will change this person's life forever.

ANN M. MARTIN lives in upstate New York near a town not unlike Camden Falls. She loves to sew and loves to take walks with her dog, Sadie. She also has three cats, Gussie, Woody, and Pippin.

Ann's acclaimed novels include *Belle Teal, A Corner of the Universe* (a Newbery Honor), *Here Today, A Dog's Life,* and *On Christmas Eve,* as well as her much-loved series The Baby-sitters Club.

To find out more about Ann, please visit www.scholastic.com/mainstreet

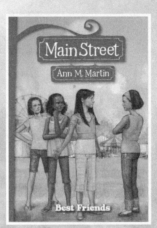
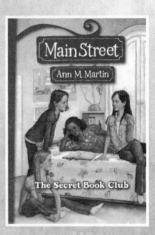